"You have the softest skin,"
Max murmured against her hair.
"Like satin."

Jessie struggled to drag air into her lungs past her constricted throat. Her eyes instinctively slid shut to better savor the sensations flowing through her.

Disoriented, she stumbled slightly as his hands tightened and he turned her around to face him.

Jessie risked a look up and was immediately lost in the swirling depths of his eyes. They seemed to glow with some emotion that her mind was too confused to decipher. She watched with an escalating hunger that threatened to consume her as his mouth came closer. Instinctively her entire body strained upward, desperate to make physical contact with him.

As his mouth brushed lightly against hers, she felt the remaining threads of her self-control snap, freeing her to move deeper into his embrace. Hunger tore through her. A hunger that was primal, drawn from the very core of who and what she was.

Dear Reader,

Just as the seasons change, you may have noticed that our Silhouette Romance covers have evolved over the past year. We have tried to create cover art that uses more soft pastels, sun-drenched images and tender scenes to evoke the aspirational and romantic spirit of this line. We have also tried to make our heroines look like women you can relate to and may want to be. After all, this line is about the joys of falling in love, and we hope you can live vicariously through these heroines.

Our writers this month have done an especially fine job in conveying this message. Reader favorite Cara Colter leads the month with *That Old Feeling* (#1814) in which the heroine must overcome past hurts to help her first love raise his motherless daughter. This is the debut title in the author's emotional new trilogy, A FATHER'S WISH. Teresa Southwick concludes her BUY-A-GUY miniseries with the story of a feisty lawyer who finds herself saddled with an unwanted and wholly irresistible bodyguard, in *Something's Gotta Give* (#1815). A sister who'd do anything for her loved ones finds her own sweet reward when she switches places with her sibling, in *Sister Swap* (#1816)— a compelling new romance by Lilian Darcy. Finally, in *Made-To-Order Wife* (#1817) by Judith McWilliams, a billionaire hires an etiquette expert to help him land the perfect society wife, and he soon starts rethinking his marriage plans.

Be sure to return next month when Cara Colter continues her trilogy and Judy Christenberry returns to the line.

Happy reading!

Ann Leslie Tuttle
Associate Senior Editor

Please address questions and book requests to:
Silhouette Reader Service
U.S.: 3010 Walden Ave., P.O. Box 1325, Buffalo, NY 14269
Canadian: P.O. Box 609, Fort Erie, Ont. L2A 5X3

MADE-TO-ORDER WIFE
Judith McWilliams

SILHOUETTE *Romance*®

Published by Silhouette Books

America's Publisher of Contemporary Romance

 SILHOUETTE BOOKS

ISBN 0-373-19817-5

MADE-TO-ORDER WIFE

Copyright © 2006 by Judith McWilliams

Books by Judith McWilliams

Silhouette Romance

Gift of the Gods #479
The Summer Proposal #1562
Her Secret Children #1648
Did You Say...Wife? #1681
Dr. Charming #1721
The Matchmaking Machine #1809
Made-To-Order Wife #1817

Silhouette Desire

Reluctant Partners #441
A Perfect Season #545
That's My Baby #597
Anything's Possible! #911
The Man from Atlantis #954
Instant Husband #1001
Practice Husband #1062
Another Man's Baby #1095
The Boss, the Beauty and the Bargain #1122
The Sheik's Secret #1228

JUDITH McWILLIAMS

began to enjoy romances while in search of the proverbial "happily-ever-after." But she always found herself rewriting the endings, and eventually the beginnings of the books she read. Then her husband finally suggested that she write novels of her own, and she's been doing it ever since.

An ex-teacher with four children, Judith has traveled the country extensively with her husband and has been greatly influenced by those experiences. While not tending the garden or caring for her family, Judith does what she enjoys most—writing. She has also written under the name of Charlotte Hines.

Dear Reader,

The idea for Jessie's occupation as a manners expert came to me one snowy late December day when my son suddenly asked, "Are there manners police?"

I glanced over to where he was sitting at the kitchen table, spared a quick look at the so far totally blank sheet of stationery in front of him and said, "Why do you ask?"

"Because I can't figure out why grown-ups would torture little kids by making them write stupid thank-you letters unless it was a law or something."

I briefly considered giving him the standard-issue mom lecture on how "if people care enough about you to run all over town tracking down an obscure toy that you said you wanted, the least you can do is write them a thank-you note," before discarding the idea. Instead, I took the easy way out and said, "Yes, there are manners police, only we call them experts, and yes, they have decreed that you can't play with your gift until you've written a thank-you note to the giver."

"But what does a manners expert look like, Mom?"

"Look like?" I repeated as into my mind suddenly popped the image of a laughing redheaded woman. To my surprise she looked exactly like the heroine of a book.

I shoved the turkey to the back of the counter, grabbed a pencil and paper and hastily started to jot her description down. And thus was born Jessie Martinelli, manners expert, whose story is told in *Made-To-Order Wife*.

I hope you enjoy reading her adventure as much as I enjoyed writing it.

Judith McWilliams

Prologue

He'd finally done it, and the proof was there in black and white for the whole world to see!

With a sense of exultation, Max Sheridan studied the article in *Forbes* that annually listed the richest Americans. For the first time his name was listed among the billionaires. Just eleven letters, but those eleven letters represented the culmination of seventeen years of single-mindedly working eighteen-hour days.

Reaching into the pants pocket of his custom-tailored gray suit, he pulled out a plain, stainless-steel key ring. Separating a small brass key, he unlocked the bottom right-hand drawer of his massive antique Regency desk. Pushing aside a pile of contracts, he pulled out a battered spiral-bound notebook. Carefully he set it on his desk and opened it to the only page that had any writing on it.

A complex swirl of remembered pain and hope engulfed him at the sight of the words penciled there. He'd been sixteen when he'd made that list of things he was going to accomplish in his life. A scared, defiant sixteen who had just buried his parents.

As he'd stood over their graves, he'd vowed that never again would he allow himself to be at the mercy of other people's decisions. And he'd kept that vow. He'd run away from the crowded foster home the state had dumped him in after his parents had died, determined to make so much money that no one would ever again have power over him.

His gaze swept the elegantly restrained grandeur of his office with its priceless antiques and original artwork, perched fifty-two stories above the bustling New York City streets. It was as far removed from the squalor he'd grown up in as he could ever imagine.

Picking up the gold fountain pen on his desk, Max deliberately drew a thick, black line through the third-to-last item on his list, which read, make a billion dollars.

His blue eyes narrowed as he studied the final two entries. Marry and have a family.

Marriage to the right woman would be the final step in his long journey toward respectability. It would be visible proof that he'd made it. That he was no longer "that woman's brat," but someone who was accepted in the highest levels of society.

Acquiring the perfect wife should be a lot like masterminding a hostile takeover in business, he reasoned. First you identified your objective and then you came up with strategies to achieve it.

He turned to a blank sheet in the notebook and, for the first time in seventeen years, began to write in it.

"Objective—wife," he wrote at the top of the page. He thought for a moment then added a slash beside the word *wife* and wrote "mother." Her role as the mother of his children would be every bit as important to him as her role as his wife.

Max stared blankly at the Monet on the wall to his right as he marshaled his thoughts.

Since he knew nothing about parenting, he was going to have to depend on his wife to show him how to recognize and nurture his children's emotional needs. She would have to teach him the basic dynamics of family life that most people instinctively absorbed during their own childhood.

Max snorted. The only insight he'd absorbed growing up was the danger of getting too close to either of his parents when they'd been drinking. That and the futility of counting on them for anything.

So, one of his most important requirements in a wife was that she have firsthand knowledge of a happy, normal childhood herself.

She should also appeal to him physically. Common sense told him that his marriage would have a better chance of success if he were sexually attracted to his wife.

An image of his last girlfriend, an internationally famous model, formed in his mind. She certainly wasn't his idea of a wife, but she definitely appealed to his libido with her tall, slender body, flawless features and long, blond hair.

Tall, blond, beautiful, he added to his list, paused, thought a moment, and then crossed out *beautiful* and substituted *attractive*. Looks weren't all that important in a wife, and he didn't want to limit his choices by being too restrictive.

Although she absolutely had to be intelligent since she was going to pass her genes on to his children. And she should be a college graduate to balance the fact that he hadn't even finished high school.

And she should like him. He didn't expect her to love

him any more than he intended to love her. In his experience, love was at best an excuse for indulging in emotional
excesses and at worst a humiliating, degrading trap.

Max winced as he recalled his father's self-pitying voice
claiming that he couldn't do anything about his wife's
flamboyantly adulterous behavior because he loved her.

No, he wanted no part of the insanity called love. Besides, from what he'd seen, marriages based on love were
very high-maintenance affairs. Women in love expected
a man to be totally wrapped up in them, and he didn't
have time for that nonsense. He was far too busy running
his business. And while he did intend to cut back on
work once his first child was born, he also intended to
spend most of his newfound free time with his children.
He was determined to be a hands-on dad. His children
were going to be the most important things in the world
to him, and he needed a wife who understood that. A wife
who wouldn't expect to be the focus of his life. A wife
who would find her emotional satisfaction in their
children and not in him. A wife who would be satisfied
with his respect and affection and not expect vows of
undying devotion.

But even if he didn't want a lot of messy emotions clut-
tering up his marriage, he also didn't want to be married
for his money. A woman whose only interest in him was
his net worth might decide to bail out at the first hint of a
problem, and a divorce accompanied by a bitter custody
battle would be devastating to his children's emotional
health. Even someone with his nonexistent parenting skills
could figure that one out.

He could protect both his children and himself to some
degree by having his future wife sign a prenup, he
decided. He added a notation to his list. A prenup wasn't

a foolproof solution to fortune hunters, but it was probably the best he could do.

And last, he wanted a wife from a socially prominent family that his children would be proud to belong to, unlike his own. He wanted his wife to reflect the fact that he'd arrived—financially and socially.

Max studied his list with a sense of satisfaction. It was the perfect blueprint for what he wanted in a wife.

But what might his prospective wife want in a husband? The unsettling thought occurred to him. Would he appeal to the kind of woman he wanted to marry? Unconsciously his fingers rubbed over the three-inch scar on his right jaw, which was the result of a barroom fight he'd gotten caught up in when he was eighteen.

Would his wealth be enough to overcome his rough-and-ready background for the type of woman he wanted to marry?

It depended, he finally decided. Depended on a lot of factors, some of which he had absolutely no control over.

And that being so, it was imperative that he seize control wherever possible. One of the things he could do would be to polish his social skills to a fine gloss. To learn to move with ease in the society his prospective wife would have been born into.

He frowned slightly as he suddenly remembered something he'd overheard at a cocktail party last month. One of the women in the group standing behind him had made a crack about Bunny Berringer, the twentysomething runway-model trophy wife of Sam Berringer, a business associate of his. Something to the effect that Bunny had undergone a transformation. That the liberal use of Sam's money had turned the socially clueless Bunny into a clone of the late Diana, Princess of Wales. But despite the women's speculation, no one had had any idea how Bunny had done it.

Max frowned slightly. While he didn't doubt that Bunny had worked hard to learn the necessary skills, someone had to have taught her what to do and when to do it. And whoever that someone was had kept his or her mouth shut or those social piranhas at the party would have heard about it.

Maybe he should talk to Sam and ask him who he'd used. He'd always gotten along well with the older man. If he explained why he needed the information... Max nodded decisively. The worst Sam could do would be to refuse to give him the information. Sam wouldn't tell anyone that he'd asked. Sam was far too smart to betray a confidence.

Picking up the phone, he asked his P.A. to get Sam on the phone. He needed to put his plan into action as soon as possible. It was already July, and he wanted to be in his own home with a wife, preferably pregnant with the first of his children, by Thanksgiving.

Chapter One

Jessie glanced down at her small gold watch as she hurried across the almost deserted lobby of the large office building toward the bank of elevators. It was one fifty-three. Perfect. She would arrive in Max Sheridan's office five minutes early. Not so early that she would seem anxious, and yet early enough that it would be clear to him that this meeting was important to her.

Stepping into an empty elevator, she pressed the button for the fifty-second floor and then checked her appearance in the mirrors that lined the elevator's walls. Her black box-pleated skirt fell almost to her knees without a wrinkle and the matching fitted jacket had no lint on it. Her gaze dropped to her long, slender legs, searching for a run in her panty hose. Thankfully, she didn't find one. Nor were there any stray specks of dirt on the highly polished gloss of her black slingback heels or her slim black briefcase.

When the unexpected summons to see the normally inaccessible head of Sheridan Electronics had come yesterday, she hadn't been sure what to wear. Normally she dressed to project an image, and the image depended on who she was working for and what she was trying to accomplish. But since she had no idea why the enigmatic Max Sheridan wanted to see her, she had finally opted for a conservative, professional look.

When the elevator opened its doors with a restrained chime on the fifty-second floor, Jessie took a deep breath, ignored the butterflies in her stomach and walked briskly toward the well-groomed middle-aged woman sitting behind an elegant antique desk in the reception area.

"I'm Jessie Martinelli," she said. "I have an appointment with Mr. Sheridan at two."

"Good afternoon, Ms. Martinelli. Just a moment while I check with his P.A. and see if he's free."

Surreptitiously Jessie looked around while the woman made the phone call. A huge cream-and-blue Aubusson carpet covered the floor, and comfortable-looking chairs had been scattered around, presumably to give the appearance of a living room in a private home. The whole area spoke of good taste and the means to indulge it.

It was the first time she'd been on the executive level of Sheridans. She'd visited their human resources department one floor down last year when she'd given a presentation on her workshops to one of their managers, but since the shortsighted woman hadn't seen the need for teaching business manners to their account executives, she'd never had a reason to return.

Could that be what this unexpected summons was about? Had they decided to use her workshops, and Max Sheridan himself wanted to discuss them? A sense of excitement tore through her. Landing an account with a conglomerate like Sheridans would do wonders for her company's bottom line.

"Mr. Sheridan will see you now, Ms. Martinelli. If you'll come with me…" The woman gave her a bright, professional smile.

Taking a deep, steadying breath, Jessie followed the receptionist.

"Ms. Martinelli, sir." The woman moved out of the open doorway, and Jessie forced herself to walk into his office, praying she didn't look as nervous as she felt. The sound of the door closing behind her echoed ominously in her ears.

Jessie instinctively tensed as the man behind the oversize mahogany desk slowly got to his feet. The office was huge, but Max Sheridan easily dominated the space. She'd seen pictures of him in the paper from time to time, but nothing had prepared her for the reality of his physical presence. He seemed to project a force field of energy that drew her like the proverbial moth to the flame.

Critically she studied him, trying to analyze her unexpected fascination with him in the hopes of minimizing its effect. He wasn't particularly tall. Probably no more than six foot, with a solid, muscular build that for some reason reminded her more of a dock worker than a business tycoon. Nor was he classically handsome. Not only were his features too bluntly chiseled, but the silvery scar on his right jaw suggested an aggressive masculinity than made mere beauty seem superfluous.

Jessie felt a tingling sensation skate over her skin as her gaze collided with his bright blue eyes. Somehow he made her aware of her femininity in a way that she'd never felt before, and she didn't like it. She was nervous enough without adding sexual tension to the mix.

Taking a deep breath, she tried a trick Maggie had taught

her years ago of picturing your audience naked, to lose your fear of them. It was a mistake. An image of Max Sheridan's broad shoulders minus the expensive gray suit jacket he had on immediately popped into her mind. His chest would probably be covered with the same inky black hair that was on his head. Would it feel as silky as his hair looked or would it feel crisp? Her fingers began to itch as if they couldn't wait to find out.

"Good morning, Ms. Martinelli." His deep, smoky voice slammed through her fantasy, smashing it to pieces— pieces that immediately reassembled themselves to form an image of him bending over her, his bare shoulders…

Stop it! She hastily sliced off her thoughts. What was the matter with her? So he had a magnetic presence. That was no excuse for her to act like some half-wit groupie. She was here on business, and she'd better start acting like the competent professional she was or she could kiss any hope of landing the Sheridan account goodbye. Max Sheridan's reputation was that he didn't tolerate incompetence. And he didn't believe in second chances.

"Mr. Sheridan." Jessie reluctantly took the hand he held out. If just being in the same room with him sent her nervous system into disarray, what would touching him be like?

Mind-blowing. She had her answer as his hand closed firmly around hers. Heat seemed to pour off his strong fingers, permeating her skin and sending her heartbeat into overdrive.

Jessie gritted her teeth, praying that the heat boiling through her wasn't visible on her face. She absolutely had to keep her professional demeanor intact.

As quickly as good manners allowed, she dropped his hand and stepped back.

"Please have a seat." Max gestured toward the chair

in front of his desk, and Jessie gingerly perched on the edge of it.

She watched as Max sat back down in his leather chair and silently studied her with a narrow-eyed intensity that made her want to get up and run. He probably wasn't even seeing her, she tried to tell herself. Chances were he'd been working on some high-powered deal when she'd arrived, and his mind was still on it.

Keeping a polite smile on her face, she waited for him to break the silence, knowing that rushing into speech would give him a tactical advantage.

Damn! Max thought in frustration as he stared at her. When he'd spoken to Sam Berringer last week, his glowing account of the fantastic job Jessie Martinelli had done in transforming his wife hadn't included a physical description: his use of words like *solid background, absolute discretion* and *unimpeachable integrity* had all suggested an older woman. He'd formed a mental image of a comfortable, grandmotherly type who was supplementing her social security check by giving etiquette lessons. And he couldn't have been more wrong. There was nothing the least bit comfortable about Jessie Martinelli.

On the contrary, there was something about her that put him on edge, and he wasn't quite sure exactly what it was. She wasn't beautiful. Her mouth was a shade too big, and her cheeks a bit too rounded. Although she did have good skin. Very soft and silky looking. He ignored his sudden compulsion to stroke it. And her eyes were intriguing. A clear, crystalline green that reminded him of emeralds. As for her hair... He studied the profusion of fiery red curls that framed her face and had an inexplicable urge to thread his fingers through them. He wanted to tug one of those curls and see how long it really was. He wanted to bury his face in the satiny mass and draw deep into his lungs the faint scent of flowers that clung to her.

For some reason that he couldn't begin to fathom, Jessie Martinelli fascinated him on a primitive level that owed nothing to rational thought.

So now what? he wondered in frustration. Did he jettison his plan because he had a totally unexpected case of the hots for his prospective consultant? But if he did that, where was he going to find someone else to help him? He could hardly advertise for an etiquette expert. It would be all over the gutter press the next day, and the last thing he wanted was publicity.

He would hire Jessie Martinelli and ignore his attraction to her, he finally decided.

"I imagine you're curious as to why I asked you to come in to see me," he said.

Max paused to allow her to say something, but she didn't. She simply gave him a small, encouraging smile and waited for him to go on. To his surprise he felt the urge to do exactly that. Jessie Martinelli had clearly mastered the technique of convincing people that she was fascinated by what they were saying.

"I want to impress on you that anything I say is to be treated with the utmost confidentiality. I would be seriously annoyed if you were to mention it to anyone else."

Jessie barely suppressed a shudder at the ice she could see glittering in his eyes. He didn't need to threaten her. Common sense told her that only a fool or a very desperate person would ever deliberately cross Max Sheridan. And she was neither.

"I understand," she said, when it became clear that he was waiting for an answer.

"I got your name from Sam Berringer. He felt you might be able to help me." He stood up as if too restless to sit still. Walking around his desk, he perched on the edge of it.

Jessie's eyes were drawn to the way the expensive material of his pants tightened over the muscles in his thighs. With an effort she dragged her eyes away from the enticing sight and forced herself to focus on his face instead. It was tense, his mouth tightly compressed.

What kind of problem did he have, she wondered, not sure she wanted to know. If it worried a man as powerful as Max Sheridan, it would probably send her screaming into the night.

Jessie had never considered it bravery to stand firm in the face of overwhelming odds. As far as she was concerned, strategy that led to debacles like the Charge of the Light Brigade was singularly stupid.

"I have reached the point in my life where I'm ready to take a new direction," he finally said. "To put it bluntly, I have decided it's time I got married and started a family."

Jessie stared blankly at him. So why was he telling her? Unless… For one mad moment she wondered if he was going to propose to her, before her common sense kicked in. He didn't know her, even if he did know about her. And men didn't propose marriage to women they'd never met. At least, normal men didn't. Although…

Unconsciously she ran the tip of her tongue over her dry lips. By no definition could Max Sheridan be called normal. Any man who rose from abject poverty to billionaire status without even the benefit of a high school education was by definition abnormal.

"Um…exactly where do I fit into your plans?" Jessie broke the silence.

"As my consultant, for want of a better word," he said.

"In what capacity?" she asked, ignoring the sharp stab of disappointment she felt.

Getting to his feet, Max walked over to the large window behind his desk. He stared down at the street far below for several moments. Then he turned and ran his long fingers through his dark hair. The action rumpled his hair, making him look younger and more approachable.

"Because of my background I don't know a lot of the finer points of social etiquette," he finally said. "I have no problem operating in a business setting. In business I know exactly what clothes and behaviors are acceptable. But on the social side, my knowledge has some gaping holes in it. Holes I need you to plug, like you did for Bunny Berringer.

"I also want you to accompany me to various social events, for two reasons. One, so you'll be on scene to offer immediate advice should it become necessary; and two, so you can listen in on conversations in places I can't go, like the women's restroom. I'm hoping what you overhear will help me to eliminate women who are simply after my money.

"In exchange, I'll pay for any clothes you'll need, plus your usual hourly rate and a bonus of fifty thousand dollars when I actually become engaged."

Max watched as her eyes widened. He'd thought the mention of a bonus would get her attention.

Attend social functions with him! Jessie tasted the words and found them very seductive. But dangerous. She was already far too aware of him. But that didn't really matter, she assured herself. What mattered was that her feelings were not reciprocated by Max. She'd seen pictures of the women he'd dated, and the only thing she had in common with them was her sex. And as for his desire to have children…

Regret shivered through her. There was no way she could ever risk having children. Not only was there the huge problem of her family's propensity for addictive behavior, but she'd probably make a ghastly mother. She might like kids in the abstract, but she had no clue about how one went about parenting them. Her own alcoholic mother certainly hadn't been a role model she could emulate.

Nevertheless, she was a sharp, competent businesswoman who could see a great opportunity staring her in the face.

Not only that, but accompanying Max to social events would put her in a position to make some valuable business contacts, because Max would do his socializing with other wealthy, influential businessmen. No matter how she looked at it, Max's proposition was a winner.

"Very well," she said. "I'll do it. Do you have a timetable?" Jessie asked.

"A timetable?"

"For implementing your plan? I imagine that you're pretty busy doing whatever it is you do."

"It's called making money," he said dryly. "I intend to delegate a lot more of my work over the next several months, while I concentrate on finding a wife. By the way, how did you get into the business of giving etiquette seminars?"

"By accident. In college I had a job at a small African embassy. I was the general gofer. During the four years I worked there, I learned a lot about formal etiquette and entertaining. When I graduated with a degree in elementary education, I couldn't get a job. So I signed up for substitute teaching and started giving seminars on etiquette to pay the bills. Somehow the business just grew, and I found

I liked the freedom of running my own company more than I liked being tied to some bureaucrat's idea of what I should be teaching."

"Serendipity. Some of my most fortunate acquisitions have come about that way," he said. "As for a timetable, I'd like to start as soon as possible."

Why the sudden hurry when, from all accounts, he'd been a perfectly content bachelor for the past thirty-three years? Jessie thought better of asking him. They might be about to embark on a very odd relationship, but when you got right down to it, she worked for him, and his personal motivation was none of her business. As for starting immediately… Mentally, she reviewed her schedule. It wasn't very full. Summers tended to be slow.

"I'm giving a workshop tonight at a local youth club on how to dress for job interviews. We could catch an early meal in a restaurant, and you could come to the workshop with me."

"Why?" Max asked.

"Because I need to observe your behavior under a variety of different situations before I can decide where to concentrate our efforts," Jessie said bluntly.

He grinned at her, and Jessie felt her breath catch at the intriguing sight of the dimple in his left cheek.

"You mean you need to find out which edges to polish?" he said.

"In a manner of speaking." With an effort, Jessie hung on to her professional detachment.

"Tonight's fine. Where do you want to eat, and what time's your workshop?"

"The workshop starts at seven-thirty, so we'll need to eat first, Mr. Sheridan. If we don't, I'll be starved by the time it's over."

"Call me Max."

"Max," Jessie obediently repeated. "Tell me—just how far are you willing to go in revamping your image?"

"I'll do whatever it takes to find the right wife," he said flatly.

Jessie shivered slightly as his face hardened in determination. She sure wouldn't want to get between him and what he wanted, she thought uneasily. It would be like trying to take a meaty bone away from a starving pit bull.

"The country-club set have some pretty rigid dress codes," she warned him. "Even when they're playing. What do you normally wear in your spare time?"

"I don't have any spare time. If I'm awake, I'm working. This will be the first time I've ever cut back. But I do have some jeans and T-shirts and sweats for working out. And one golfing outfit," he added.

"I suggest that you pay a visit to wherever you buy your suits and pick out some casual clothes."

"I have a better idea. We'll both pay a visit to my tailor, and you can make suggestions," he said.

"I'm free tomorrow morning—say, ten? What about where you live? A good address is very important to a lot of people. Your future wife might be among them. Although, with as much money as you have, we could always try passing you off as eccentric." She frowned slightly as she considered the idea. "It's too bad you aren't an actor."

"An actor! Why would a sane person want to be one of the Hollywood crowd?"

"Because no one seems to hold them to the normal rules of behavior."

"*That* is blatantly obvious. But forget passing me off as eccentric."

"You're probably right," she said. "There's a thin line

between eccentric and just plain weird, and it's too easy to inadvertently cross it. Where do you live?"

"I have an apartment on East Seventy-Fourth, and a town house I picked up last year, which I was told would be suitable for a family. As I recall, it has over fourteen thousand square feet."

Jessie blinked. Fourteen thousand square feet! Just how big a family was he planning?

"Where is it?" she asked.

"I don't know."

Jessie stared at him. "You bought a house, and you don't remember where it is!"

"I never actually saw it. It was part of a package deal in a company acquisition. My business manger said it had a lot of potential."

Jessie shuddered.

"What's the matter?"

"Words like *potential* and *quaint* are terms to avoid when buying property."

"You think?" he asked.

"I know. I have a friend in real estate, and I've listened to her write copy on occasion. Real estate ads definitely come under the heading of creative fiction."

"I'll get the address and the key from my lawyer, and we can stop and look it over tomorrow after we order my casual wardrobe. If you think it wouldn't appeal to a woman, then I'll find something else."

"Okay," she said, suppressing an envious sigh at the thought of being wealthy enough to simply go out and buy a piece of New York City.

"Also, I have an invitation to a cocktail party this Friday night at Edwin Biddle's," he continued. "I'd like to start my search for a wife there. You are free Friday night, aren't you?"

Jessie bit back the urge to tell him that just because he didn't fancy her didn't mean she didn't have a social life. This was business, she reminded herself. Potentially very profitable business. Until she managed to get him engaged, her own social life, such as it was, was going to have to be put on hold.

"As long as it's just a cocktail party, it should be okay."

"You like cocktail parties?" he asked curiously.

"It's not that. It's that I won't have time to teach you much by Saturday, but you've probably had plenty of practice at cocktail parties. It may be trite, but it's also true that you only get one chance to make a good first impression."

"I'll keep that in mind. I'll also pick you up tonight at six."

Jessie got to her feet, correctly assuming she'd just been dismissed.

"Six will be fine. And please don't change."

Max frowned slightly. "Why not?"

"Because I want the kids to see what a real employer looks like. In fact, you can give a couple of practice interviews, if you would," she said hopefully.

"All right, but be warned that I haven't interviewed anyone for an entry-level job in fifteen years.

"Until tonight, then." Max held his office door open for her, and Jessie hurried through, feeling as if she were escaping from a relentless force of nature.

She didn't begin to relax until she was safely outside the building on the sidewalk. She spent the bus ride home trying to sort out her impressions of Max Sheridan and the job she'd taken on. Having met him, she wasn't surprised at his unorthodox method of choosing a wife instead of waiting for love to strike as most men would.

Jessie frowned, trying to remember if he'd said anything about love. She was almost positive he hadn't. Did that mean he didn't expect to find love in his marriage? Or did it mean that he didn't think his emotions were any of her business? It could be either. Or neither. She had no way of knowing.

But even if his marriage started out as a cold-blooded bargain, she very much doubted that it would stay that way for long. She swallowed as she remembered the sensual line of his mouth, and the strength in his long fingers as they had gripped hers. Max Sheridan was a compulsively attractive man, and his attraction owed nothing to his net worth.

Jessie got off at her bus stop and walked down the block to her apartment house.

Letting herself into the lobby, she picked up her mail and sorted through it on the elevator ride up to her apartment on the fourth floor. She bypassed the bills and flyers in favor of a pale-pink envelope with her address neatly typed on it. Curiously, Jessie studied the uneven keystrokes. It looked as if it had been typed on a typewriter and not a computer.

Ripping it open, she pulled out a single sheet of pink stationery. When she saw the handwriting, a volatile mix of pain and anger swamped her, making her want to throw up.

She closed her eyes and took several deep breaths, willing her stomach to behave. When she finally felt marginally in control, she forced herself to read the words on the paper. What she really wanted to do was rip it to shreds and then stomp on the pieces.

The elevator doors opened and she got out, automatically heading toward her apartment, her movements feeling stiff and unnatural.

Once she was inside, she went into the kitchen to put on a pot of coffee. She desperately needed a strong shot of caffeine to counteract the shock she'd just had.

Kicking off her heels, she set the letter in the middle of her gray granite countertop and then stood there, staring down at it as if it were a snake about to strike.

"Damn!" she muttered. "How could she write to me? And why now? Why not last year when she first got out of prison?"

Too agitated to sit still, Jessie began to pace as she waited for her coffee to brew. She didn't want to hear from her mother. They didn't have any good memories to share. Not a single solitary one. Thanks to her mother's alcoholism, Jessie had had a childhood straight out of a Kafka nightmare. And now her mother had the nerve to write to her and suggest meeting, as if nothing had ever happened.

Hell would freeze over before she'd ever have anything to do with her mother again, Jessie thought grimly. She had built her own life. It was a good life. A normal life. And there was no place in it for her mother's destructive presence.

No place at all.

Chapter Two

Jessie tensed, automatically checking the kitchen clock when she heard the entrance buzzer sound. Exactly six o'clock. It had to be Max. Anticipation poured through her, jerking her to her feet.

Hastily she shoved her feet into her black slingbacks, wincing slightly as the fashionable shoes pinched her toes. Someday she was going to have enough money to retire somewhere peaceful and rural where she'd never wear anything but comfortable walking shoes again.

As she grabbed her purse off the counter, the pale-pink letter lying there caught her eye. Why had her mother written? Was she hoping to con Jessie into paying for her liquor? A surge of anger coursed through her as she remembered how her mother used to steal her babysitting money to buy alcohol. She'd been there and done that and she wasn't going back. Not ever again.

All she had to do was to stand firm, she told herself as

she got into the elevator and punched the button for the lobby. Once her mother realized that she wouldn't allow herself to be used, she'd go away. At least, Jessie sure hoped she would.

The elevator came to its usual jerky stop on the ground floor, and Jessie stepped out. Her breath caught in her lungs as she caught sight of Max standing on the street outside. Even through the thick plate glass of the door she could see the impatient glitter in his blue eyes. As if he had worlds to conquer, and she was delaying him.

Max watched Jessie cross the small lobby toward him. Her face was composed and remote as if her mind was far away, occupied with more important things that having dinner with him. For some reason her preoccupation annoyed him. He wanted to swing her up in his arms, find the nearest bed and make love to her until she lost that infuriating aura of self-control that she radiated.

And the fact that he knew he couldn't act on his sexual attraction for her only made it worse. Maybe what they said about forbidden fruit really was true, he thought wryly. Maybe it really did taste sweeter.

Hopefully his reaction to Jessie Martinelli would fade as quickly as it had appeared. It was much too intense not to burn itself out relatively quickly. All he had to do was to keep his mind firmly focused on what she could do to help him achieve his goals.

Praying the excitement she felt wasn't visible in her face, Jessie pushed open the street door and stepped out into the warm summer evening.

"Hi," she said, trying her best to sound impersonally pleasant.

Max gave her a brisk nod and said, "I've got reservations for six-fifteen at a restaurant not too far from here. I brought the car since taxi service can be chancy at this time of night."

Jessie glanced at the shiny black Mercedes parked at the curb. Its dark, impenetrable windows added to its air of aloofness. The car fit him perfectly. Both were elegant, solidly built and expensive, with an underlying power that could squash the unwary.

"You get points for being on time." She hoped that focusing on the reason why they were together would dampen the excessive pleasure she felt in his company.

"Don't tell me. Promptness really is a virtue?"

"It's also becoming very rare," she said.

"I refuse to waste my time waiting for people to show up, so I extend the same courtesy to others."

"A commendable attitude," she murmured, surprised at his words. Most of the high-powered businessmen she worked with saw nothing wrong with keeping small-business people like herself waiting indefinitely to see them.

"I'm glad you approve," he said dryly.

Taking her arm, he headed toward the car and opened the rear door. Hurriedly she climbed into the car and scooted across the leather seat to make room for Max.

"Jessie, this is Fred. Fred, Ms. Martinelli," Max said, introducing his driver.

"Evening, Ms. Martinelli." Fred pulled into traffic with a deft turn of the powerful car's steering wheel.

"Good evening, Fred," Jessie said, wondering how long Fred had worked for Max and how well he knew him. This job had one interesting side benefit. She had the perfect excuse to ask all kinds of questions that normally would be considered none of her business.

Unfortunately, the most burning question she had was one Max couldn't answer, and that was why she reacted to him like he was the embodiment of her every masculine fantasy when her mind knew perfectly well he wasn't. Her fantasies had always been about lean, debonair, sophisticated men. Maybe it was a result of her passion for vintage black-and-white movies, but from the time she'd been old enough to understand what sexual attraction was all about, her physical ideal had been men like Cary Grant or Sir Laurence Olivier. Sometimes she had the feeling that she'd been born out of time. She would have been much happier back in the twenties.

"I have reservations at a restaurant called Saretts. Have you been there before?" Max asked, curious about where her dates normally took her. If this were a real date, he'd take her to a five-star restaurant for dinner. Followed by a Broadway show and afterward he'd…

"No, I've never heard of it," Jessie said. "Which is hardly surprising. Sometimes I think New York is wall-to-wall restaurants."

Did that mean that she ate at a lot of them? Max wondered. And if she did, did she go with someone? A male someone?

"I intend to monopolize your time over the next six weeks or so. I hope no one will be upset."

"No." To his annoyance Jessie deflected his question without telling him anything. *No* could mean anything. It could mean that she was involved with someone who was willing to put up with her heavy workload. Or it could mean that she wasn't involved with anyone on a personal level at the moment. Max felt an intense surge of frustration engulf him at his lack of any real personal information about her. Sam had rhapsodized for twenty minutes about her competence, her trustworthiness, her ethics and her solid record for results, but at no time in the conversation had he said anything about her personal life other than the fact that she had never done anything that would leave her open to blackmail.

"Here we are, sir," Fred announced as he pulled up in front of the restaurant.

He could slip in a few personal questions over dinner, Max decided. He'd never found it particularly hard to get a woman talking. In fact, usually he couldn't get them to shut up.

"I'll page you when I want to be picked up, Fred," Max said as the driver opened his door. Outside, he waited while Jessie got out, then took her arm and began walking.

"Is Fred the modern-day equivalent of an old family retainer?" Jessie asked.

"No. There is nothing old-fashioned about Fred. He comes from a security firm that specializes in drivers who know how to kill in unarmed combat."

Jessie stopped dead on the sidewalk and stared at him in shock. "He what?"

"There are a lot of dangerous people out there, and a wise man takes precautions."

Jessie shivered at the reminder of just how perilous the world had become, and at Max's casual attitude toward it. "I never thought of it before, but there are distinct advantages in not having much money. Have you been threatened?"

"No, but I started taking precautions after an Italian friend of mine was kidnapped last year. Kidnapping seems to be a way of life in Italy these days, and I do a lot of business over there."

"What happened?" Jessie asked.

"His son and I rescued him. We couldn't take the risk they'd let him go after the ransom was paid."

Opening the door, he ushered her into the restaurant. Despite it being early, the place was almost full.

"I have reservations for two under the name of Sheridan."

"Of course, Mr. Sheridan." The hostess gave him a bright, professional smile. "If you'll just follow me."

The woman led them to a booth set along the wall opposite the front window, and Jessie slipped into the plush velvet seat.

"Your waitperson will be with you shortly." The hostess handed them each a menu and then left.

Jessie opened the menu and then asked, "Do you normally open doors for women?"

Max looked at her in surprise. "Why? Is there something wrong with that?" he asked.

"Manners aren't a question of right and wrong," Jessie said. "Think of them as the grease that lubricates the friction of living in close proximity with other people. As far as I'm concerned, having a man open doors for me is a plus. However, some women feel that a man doing something for them that they can do for themselves is patronizing. It will turn them off. If you want to marry a woman who thinks like that, then you need to practice letting women open their own doors."

Max stared off in the middle distance for a long moment and said, "Opening doors for women is just habit. I grew up in the South, and manners there tend to be a bit more traditional. But I have no real opinion either way."

"Good," Jessie said. "Once you focus in on a woman you intend to court, you can simply follow her lead."

"Yes," Max said as he tried to imagine what his final choice would look like. But the only image that formed in his mind was of Jessie. Proximity, he told himself.

"What would you like to eat?" Max asked.

"I'm still thinking about it," she said.

"Well, think faster. The waitress will be here in a minute."

"Waitperson. Political correctness is very important with the social crowd you'll be moving in. Or, at least, lip service to it is."

Max eyed the waitress serving the couple at a table about ten feet from them. "My imagination isn't equal to the task of thinking of someone like her in sexless terms," he said.

Jessie turned to follow his gaze and found herself staring at a tall blonde wearing slim black pants that highlighted her long, slender legs and a white blouse that fitted snuggly over her well-developed breasts.

As Jessie watched, the woman turned slightly and aimed a dazzling white smile at the man at the next table. Not only was the woman built like a Playboy centerfold, but she was gorgeous, too.

"I see the problem." Jessie tried to get a handle on her own feeling of inferiority in the face of such blatant feminine perfection.

"Is that what you envision your future wife looking like?" Jessie asked.

Max took a second look at the waitress, his eyes lingering on the sexy pout of her collagen-enhanced lips. He tried to imagine her holding a wiggling toddler in her arms and failed utterly. She'd probably be too afraid the kid would mess up her hair. Even worse, she'd undoubtedly object to spoiling her figure by having a baby in the first place.

"Not particularly," he said. "Besides, beautiful women tend to be very high maintenance. Over the long haul that would get real old real fast. And marriage is for the long haul."

"You wouldn't know it to look at the divorce statistics these days. Half of all marriages fail."

Max studied the somber shadows in her eyes, wondering what had put them there. Could she have been married herself and gone through a messy divorce?

"Look at the bright side. That means that half of all marriages are a success," he said.

Jessie grinned at him, and Max had the oddest feeling that he'd just stepped out of the shadows into brilliant sunlight.

"Let me guess," she said. "You're one of those people who see the glass half full instead of half empty?"

"No, I'm one of those people who immediately starts negotiating for water rights so I don't have to worry."

Jessie's grin dissolved into a chuckle. "Practicality is so much more appealing."

"Not to everyone," he muttered, remembering his last girlfriend's numerous complaints about his lack of romantic gestures. "Some women infinitely prefer the romantic approach."

"But what's romantic varies depending on whom you're talking to. Personally, I think a man who can provide the necessities of life is very romantic, but then, I'm willing to admit that I have a practical bent of mind. You just need to find a woman who thinks like you do."

"You don't believe in opposites attracting?" Max asked.

Pain speared through her as she remembered her mother's many lovers. "Take it from one who has been there, it's much too risky. Offbeat habits that seem endearing at the beginning can become major stumbling blocks later on."

"I'll have the Dijon chicken with a tossed salad, house dressing on the side, and a glass of white wine," Jessie said, changing the subject as the waitress approached their table.

Surreptitiously Jessie studied the waitress's perfect fea-

tures, searching for a flaw. She couldn't find one. If anything the woman looked better up close than she did from
a distance.

Jessie tensed as the woman addressed Max by name.

"I'm so honored to meet you, Mr. Sheridan." The
woman gave him an adoring look that made Jessie want to
gag. "I've seen your picture in the paper many times, but
I never thought I'd get to meet you in person." She gave a
throaty laugh that Jessie would have been willing to bet she
practiced three times a day in front of a mirror.

Jessie ignored such blatant behavior in favor of watching
how Max responded to the woman. To her surprise he didn't
react. At least, not outwardly. He simply nodded as if to ac-
knowledge her words, and proceeded to order.

Undaunted by his reserved manner, the waitress continued to flirt with him. Almost as if she couldn't believe that
he wasn't captivated by her looks.

When she finally left, Jessie said, "Well done."

He shot her a sharp glance and said, "What do you mean?"

"I mean how you resisted the impulse to respond to her
blatant come-on while with another woman, even if that
woman is simply a business colleague."

Max's smile held a cynical edge that chilled Jessie. "It
wasn't hard. She wasn't flirting with me. She was flirting
with my money."

Jessie frowned. "What makes you say that?"

"She knew my name," he said flatly. "In my position you
learn to recognize the obvious hangers-on. It saves a lot of
trouble in the long run."

"I guess. So how do you tell if someone likes you for
yourself?"

"I don't. That's why I need you to listen in on my prospective wife's conversations for me. Hopefully, your

input will give me a better idea of what a woman really thinks about me."

The bleak expression that suddenly darkened his eyes to navy tore at her heart. For a second he had looked so alone. So terribly alone. As if he didn't have a friend in the world. Which was ridiculous, she told herself. Max was a fascinating man. He probably had lots of friends, and despite what he obviously believed, she didn't have the slightest doubt that he'd attract women in droves even if he didn't have a dime to his name. He'd simply attract a different type of woman. Women who, in her opinion, were probably worth a whole lot more than the fortune hunters after him now.

She leaned back in the seat as the young man who'd been tending bar brought them their drinks, gave them a harried smile and hurried back to the bar.

Jessie sipped the excellent white wine and then asked, "What about religion?"

Max eyed her narrowly. "You can't be a religious fanatic, because you're drinking alcohol."

"My religious beliefs are irrelevant. Yours aren't. Do you have any religious requirements in a wife?"

Max thought about it for a moment and then said, "No specific requirements, but children need the stability of going to church on Sunday."

"No, children need the stability to being *taken* to church on Sunday," Jessie corrected him. "What's more, if you're going to join a church, you'd better be prepared to live up to the teaching of whatever denomination you choose, because nothing will mess kids up quicker than being exposed to hypocrisy."

Max blinked at her acerbic tone. "That caveat sounds very personal. What happened? Did your parents let you down?"

"No," Jessie said, telling herself that it wasn't exactly a lie. Her mother's behavior had been absolutely predictable. She'd make promise after promise. Big promises such as she'd quit drinking, and little promises such as she'd come to Jessie's school's open house. And her mother had broken every one of them. Without fail.

To Jessie's relief the waitress arrived with their salads, distracting Max. She was going to have to be careful to keep a tight rein on her responses, she realized. Max was a very astute man. She didn't want him curious about her background. If he were to find out just how bad it was, he might decide she wasn't the right person for the job of steering him through the tricky shoals of his courtship. A feeling of panic swelled in her at the thought of Max firing her. But only because she really wanted the bonus he'd promised, she assured herself. To say nothing of the fact that she was looking forward to making some very useful business contacts. The social circles Max was going to take her into should be teeming with potential clients.

As Jessie ate, she surreptitiously watched Max. To her relief, he had perfect table manners. She wouldn't have to teach him the basics like she tended to have to do with a lot of the new college hires in her workshops.

"What's the verdict?" Max asked as he set his napkin down.

"Verdict?" Jessie repeated.

"You've been watching me like a hawk through the entire meal. Did I pass muster?"

"Yes." Jessie saw no reason to lie about what she'd been doing. "Have you attended many formal dinners?"

"No. I avoid them like the plague."

"Then you probably haven't been exposed to things like fish forks and the like. We'll go over fancy place settings and exotic silverware to make sure you have them down pat before you get in too deep with the country-club set."

"We," he corrected. "Don't forget, you're coming along as my on-scene consultant."

Jessie felt an odd mixture of anticipation and foreboding swirl through her. "I haven't forgotten," she said.

"Do you want dessert?" he asked.

"No, thanks. We don't have time. Since one of the things I stress to the kids is the absolute necessity of being on time for a job, it would hardly look good if I were to show up late."

"All right." Max pulled his pager out of his pocket, pushed the button and then gestured toward the waitress, who was keeping them under surveillance.

The woman arrived at their table so fast it was a wonder she didn't leave skid marks on the floor, Jessie thought acidly.

"May I have the check?" Max asked her.

"Certainly, Mr. Sheridan." With a sultry smile the woman handed him a small leather folder containing the bill and left.

Max opened it, looked it over and then dropped several bills on it.

Jessie's eyes narrowed as she noticed the white piece of paper on the side opposite the bill. It appeared to have a name and phone number written on it. The waitress's? A flash of rage sizzled through Jessie. How dare that blasted woman try to pick up Max while he was with another woman?

"Coming?" Max said as he got to his feet, trying not to let his annoyance show at the way Jessie kept retreating into her thoughts.

Jessie hurriedly got to her feet and followed him out of the restaurant, inordinately glad that he had left the paper with the waitress's name and number on the table.

Fred and the Mercedes were double-parked at the curb, and Jessie quickly climbed into the backseat.

"Evening, Fred," she greeted the taciturn driver.

"Evening, Ms.," he said absently as his eyes continuously swept the area around the car.

"I feel like someone should yell lights, camera, action," she muttered.

"Fred takes security very seriously," Max said.

"Damn right I do," Fred said flatly as he pulled out into traffic. "Where to?"

"Jessie?"

Jessie gave him the address of the youth club.

"Not the best neighborhood," Fred said in obvious disapproval.

"Not the worst, either," Jessie said.

"We'll be fine, Fred," Max said. "Don't worry."

Jessie shot a quick look at Max out of the corner of her eye, her gaze lingering on the firm line of his lips, and longing welled through her.

Max might be fine, but she was beginning to have serious doubts about herself.

Chapter Three

"If I had money, I sure as hell wouldn't want no job."

"I see." Max studied the short, thin teenager sprawled in the chair in front of him.

"And I tell you, man, it ain't all that much money to start with." Luis shoved his fingers through his overlong black hair. "Nobody pays much over the minimum."

"Somehow, I'm not surprised," Max said dryly.

He glanced over his shoulder at Jessie, who was sitting in the back of the room, watching the interview with a serene expression. She gave him an encouraging smile that inexplicably warmed him.

"Luis," Jessie said, "you should never, ever tell a prospective employer that you only want a job for the money."

Luis gave her a disbelieving look. "Nobody's dumb enough to believe that I'm working for the fun of it, Jessie."

"I know, but it's just one of those things that you don't say," she continued with the same unflagging patience she'd shown all evening.

She'd make a great mother, Max thought idly. She'd never lose her air of calm competence no matter how annoying her kids got. Her kids wouldn't have to learn to duck flying fists the way he had.

"It's like when your girlfriend asks you if you think she's gained weight," Jessie said. "You wouldn't be stupid enough to say yes, would you, even if it's obvious she has?"

Luis scowled as he considered her words. "Guess not," he muttered. Clearly it was a comparison he could relate to.

"If I ain't supposed to tell the truth, Jessie, what kind of lie do I tell 'em?" Luis finally asked.

"Whatever half-truth works to get your foot in the door," Max said.

"Max Sheridan!" Jessie yelped. "You can't tell him that."

"Wrong. I not only can, I just did."

"But that's dishonest," she said.

"No, that's the way the game is played. The only caveat, and it's an important one, is never claim to be able to do something you can't do or to have credentials you don't have. Sooner or later an outright lie will trip you out, and then your credibility will be in the toilet."

"I do whatever I gotta," Luis said.

"Why do you want a job so much?" Max asked, and then wished he hadn't. He most definitely didn't want to get any more involved with Jessie's strays. He'd already wasted most of an evening when he could have been focusing on his own concerns. He stole a quick sideways glance at Jessie to find her studying Luis with a worried expression on her face. Max frowned. He didn't want her thinking about anything but finding him a wife.

"To buy food. My ma was operated on 'cause a couple of her arteries was blocked, but she can't go back to work for months yet. The company she works for says she's gotta be outta work for six months before she can get disability, and the government takes months and months to get welfare. And what's m'little brothers supposed to eat till then...." Luis gulped as if trying to slow down the torrent of words pouring out of him. "I went to the food pantry over at the church, and they gave me some stuff, but they said they ain't got enough for everybody who needs it. What they did give me ain't nothing like what that nurse said Ma was supposed to be eating."

Max winced as he saw the stark fear that momentarily peeped out from behind Luis's tough-guy facade. He didn't bother to ask where Luis's father was. He knew the statistics.

For a moment Max remembered how he'd felt at seventeen, scared and defiant with no place to go and no one to turn to for help. But at least he hadn't been responsible for anyone else.

"Then my friend Stuts told me 'bout how Jessie was having this thing tonight, so I came."

"What kind of skills do you have?" Max asked.

"Whatcha mean?"

"What can you do that an employer would be willing to pay you money for?" Max rephrased.

"I do anything. Ain't particular. Just don't want to get caught," Luis said.

"Come by my office first thing tomorrow morning and we'll fix you up with something." Max heard the words emerge from his mouth with a feeling of disbelief.

"Really, man?" Luis eyed him with hope heavily tinged with suspicion.

"Really." Max squashed his doubts with a monumental effort. Hiring one of Jessie's social misfits wouldn't be that big a deal, he told himself. Human Resources would find him something to do in a quiet corner, and Max would never hear from or about him again.

Max reached into his jacket pocket and pulled out his wallet. He took out a business card, jotted a note to his Human Resources manager on it and then handed it and a folded hundred-dollar bill to Luis.

"The money is an advance on your salary," Max told him. "It will be deducted from your first paycheck. Take the card to Human Resources, and they'll find you a job."

Luis snatched up the card and the bill almost as if he was afraid that Max might try to take it back. Jumping to his feet, he backed toward the door. "Thanks, man. Thanks, Jessie." He ducked his head as if embarrassed and then bolted through the door.

"Why did you do that?" she asked uncertainly. "You didn't offer a job to the other kids you interviewed and without a doubt, Luis is the most hopeless one of the lot."

"Maybe he's got hidden qualities." Max rubbed the back of his neck, not wanting to admit that he'd done it because, for an instant, he'd seen his own youthful self in Luis's panicked eyes. If Jessie thought he was a soft touch, she'd be after him to employ more of her lame ducks.

He watched as Jessie headed to the desk in the front of the room to get her notes. She had the most graceful walk, he thought. As if she were moving to music that only she could hear.

"How often do you volunteer down here?" he asked, using words to try to quell his instinctive reaction to her. "Most of the kids seem to know you by name."

"I'm here three to four times a week. Mostly I tutor in the after-school program for the younger kids. There's never enough money to pay for staff.

"Tell me, where do you visualize Luis fitting into your organization?" she asked.

"Fortunately, that's not my problem. It's for Human Resources. But I'm warning you right now, whether or not he keeps the job is up to him."

Jessie grimaced. "I hope Luis is up to the challenge. He doesn't have much experience to call on, and he certainly doesn't have any role models at home."

"If Luis wants to keep the job, he'll learn fast. If he doesn't, he won't, and he'll be history," Max said flatly. "I'm willing to give him a hand up, but I won't give him a handout."

Jessie studied Max's eyes, looking for signs of softness, but she couldn't find any. He appeared to mean exactly what he said. But he had given Luis that hundred-dollar bill, and he had to know that there was a good chance he'd never see either Luis or his hundred dollars again. So Max couldn't be as hard as he was trying to appear. He had to have a softer side. He just kept it very well hidden.

"Are we done here?" Max's voice broke into her thoughts.

"Yes. Luis was the last."

Pulling his pager out of his pocket, Max summoned Fred and then took her arm, steering her toward the center's front entrance.

Jessie felt the warmth from his fingers through the thin material of the jacket she was wearing, and she shivered. What was it about this man's touch that affected her so? she wondered uneasily.

"What time should I pick you up tomorrow morning?" Max's deep voice broke into her muddled thoughts.

"Tomorrow?" she repeated blankly.

Max looked down into her confused features, feeling a

flash of annoyance at her preoccupied expression. For what he was paying her she would damn well keep her attention firmly focused on him.

"We're scheduled to acquire my casual wardrobe and then to inspect the townhouse I own."

"That's right. The one you don't know the address of."

"Didn't. My lawyer sent a key and the location over to my office late this afternoon."

"Good," Jessie said. "Where shall I meet you?"

"I'll pick you up at your apartment. Say, ten o'clock?"

"Ten is fine," Jessie said as she followed him out of the youth center. By tomorrow she should have regained her sense of equilibrium and would be able to view Max Sheridan as just one more client. At least, she certainly hoped so.

Jessie's first sight of Max as she emerged from her apartment building the following morning shattered her hopes. He was wearing a pair of worn black jeans that molded his flat hips and muscular thighs like a second skin. After one covetous glance that sent her body temperature skyrocketing, Jessie jerked her gaze up past the black T-shirt stretched across his broad chest to land on his face.

She swallowed convulsively as she felt her mouth water. He was the most enticing sight she'd seen in years. He looked like he'd strayed out of that vintage James Dean movie she'd watched last week. All he needed to complete the image was a Harley-Davidson Hog instead of the big black Mercedes waiting at the curb.

"Why would I want a motorcycle?" he asked, and Jessie winced when she realized she must have spoken out loud. What was it about Max that sent her brain into idiot mode?

"To go with the rest of your outfit," she said, and hurriedly changed the subject. "What men's store are we going to?"

"Atkins. Over by Saks. It's where I get my suits."

Max opened the Mercedes door for her, and she quickly got inside.

"Good morning, Fred," Jessie said.

"Morning, Ms. Martinelli," Fred responded without ever taking his eyes off his surveillance of the street.

Max climbed in behind her and slammed the door closed with a well-engineered thud.

"Put on your seat belt," Max ordered as Fred deftly pulled out into traffic.

"The way Fred keeps checking for villains I feel like I ought to stay unbuckled so I can make a quick getaway if I have to."

"Fasten your seat belt," Max repeated. "You know New York City traffic is dangerous."

"All right." Jessie pushed aside her cream linen blazer and buckled the belt around her slim beige chinos. "Satisfied?"

Satisfied? Max's eyes dropped to her soft pink lips and a shaft of desire twisted through him as he imagined what they would feel like beneath his. No, he damn well wasn't satisfied. But mixing business with pleasure almost never worked. A sense of regret shimmered through him.

"What am I going to buy?" he said, forcing himself to focus on why they were together.

"If that's a sample of your casual clothes, everything," she said bluntly.

Max glanced down at his T-shirt. "You don't like it? It's my favorite."

"And has been for most of your adult life, judging by its threadbare condition," she said tartly.

"Waste not, want not," Max intoned piously.

"What does that have to do with anything?"

"Nothing. I just thought it sounded good. Fiscally responsible and all that."

"Forget it. You don't want to say anything that might give your future wife the idea that you're cheap. Cheap husbands are the pits."

"There's a big difference between fiscally responsible and cheap," Max insisted. "Besides, how would you know? Were you married to a cheapskate once?" He slipped the question in.

"I've never been married to anyone, no matter what their fiscal outlook," Jessie said. "But I've listened to enough stories from girlfriends to be able to imagine the rest. I suppose…"

She broke off as Fred pulled up in front of Atkins.

They were intercepted the moment they walked inside the shop. Almost as if the salesman didn't want to let them contaminate his premises, Jessie thought wryly.

"May I help you?" The salesman glanced at Max, winced and then hastily refocused on Jessie.

"No," Max said flatly, and the man instinctively took a step backward from the authority that resonated in Max's deep voice.

"Just looking." Jessie softened Max's flat rejection.

"Supercilious bastard!" Max muttered when the man moved away.

"I think his attitude comes under the heading of servants being bigger snobs than their employers," Jessie said. "Now, first we need…"

"Mr. Sheridan!" A delighted-sounding voice accosted them from the rear of the shop. "How may I be of assistance to you?"

Jessie turned to find an elderly man hurriedly limping toward them. "Was there a problem with any of the suits we sent you?"

"Not at all. I simply find myself in need of some casual clothes," Max said.

"I can't tell you how pleased I am that you've chosen us to outfit you," the man said, and then turned to smile charmingly at Jessie.

"This is Jessie Martinelli, my corporate-image consultant. Jessie, Mr. Atkins."

"Mr. Atkins." Jessie shook the man's hand.

"And a very nice image she presents, too." Mr. Atkins nodded approvingly at the chic simplicity of her outfit.

"What do you want to buy, Mr. Sheridan?"

"What do I want?" Max turned to Jessie.

"Outfits suitable for casual weekends at house parties," Jessie said. "And golfing clothes, tennis whites and some boating outfits."

"I learned to golf because a lot of business takes place on the golf course, but I've never even been on a tennis court, and the closest I've been to a boat was a raft I built as a kid. It sank two feet from shore," Max said wryly.

"Minor details," Jessie said. Turning to Mr. Atkins, she said, "Basically, we want to be prepared for any casual eventuality."

"Maybe we ought to just buy the store," Max muttered. Jessie ignored him.

Mr. Atkins turned and looked Max over with the intensity of a professional tailor. "That should present no problem. Fortunately, Mr. Sheridan is a standard size. Everything is in stock. If you'll come with me, you can try on…"

"No." Max flatly rejected the suggestion. "I don't need

to try anything on. We'll just pick out what I need, and you can send it on to my apartment."

"Of course, Mr. Sheridan," Mr. Atkins agreed, before Jessie could say anything. "If for some reason something doesn't fit, call us and we'll come get it and bring another size."

Jessie sighed enviously. Shopping sure was easy if you were worth a billion dollars.

Thirty minutes later, they had accumulated an impressive collection of clothes.

"I'll never wear all those," Max complained as Jessie was unable to resist adding a gorgeous cobalt-blue cashmere sweater to the pile. It exactly matched his eyes.

"Sure you will," Jessie insisted.

"That will do for the moment," Jessie told Mr. Atkins. "Would you please leave one of the sets of tennis gear out? We want to take it with us."

"Certainly." Mr. Atkins picked up a pair of white shorts and a white polo and put them into one of the store's distinctive black-and-gold carrier bags. "There you are. We'll deliver the rest of your purchases this afternoon."

"Thanks." Max accepted the bag, took Jessie's arm and rushed her toward the door as if he were escaping the scene of a robbery.

"What's your hurry?" she demanded as she skipped to keep up with him.

"I want to get you out of here before you realize that there are still one or two things left in the store that we haven't bought yet."

"Remember what I said about only getting one chance to make a good first impression."

"The only thing you've made an impression on this morning is my wallet," he said dryly.

Jessie frowned as she watched Max page Fred. "Come to think of it, we left before you signed for all that stuff."

"I have an account here. Atkins'll send me an itemized bill. What are we going to do with the tennis clothes?"

"I'm going to give you a tennis lesson this afternoon."

Max glanced down at her in surprise. "You play tennis?"

"Quite well, as a matter of fact," she said with no false modesty. "It's a good sport for someone who lives in the city, because it doesn't take much equipment, and you can play indoors year round."

"I don't like organized sports," Max said, remembering his father's insistence that he play football and how much he'd hated it.

"Two people batting a ball back and forth can hardly be called organized anything. I'll set up a lesson on sailing for you if you tell me when you're available."

She hurried forward as Fred pulled up, double-parking in front of the store.

Once they were safely inside the car, she asked, "So when will it be convenient? We don't want to wait too long. It should take a while to become moderately competent."

"How about if we rent a sailboat and you can give me instructions?" Max suggested.

"Sorry, I don't sail," she said. "There are less strenuous and far cheaper ways to get a sunburn."

"Then you can come along and learn with me."

"Not a good idea. I can't swim."

"You can't swim!" Max looked at her in shock.

"Hell, lady, you'd be easy to kill," Fred observed from the front seat. "Just drop you in some deep water and let nature take its course."

"Fortunately, no one wants to kill me," Jessie said tartly.

"You really can't swim?" Max asked.

"I really can't swim. I never learned as a child and have never had the time or the inclination as an adult."

"Everyone should know how to swim," Max said.

"Statements that start with 'everyone should' annoy the hell out of me!"

"I'll give you a lesson this afternoon, right after you teach me tennis," Max said.

"Thanks for the thought, but I have absolutely no desire whatsoever to learn to swim."

"I don't want to learn to play tennis," Max shot back, "but I will because it's in my best interests. Just like it's in your best interests to learn to swim."

"He's right, Ms. Martinelli." Fred threw in his two cents' worth.

"We'll discuss this later," Jessie muttered, having the feeling she was being ganged up on.

"Where is the town house?" She determinedly changed the subject as Fred headed up Fifth Avenue.

"It's on East Sixty-Fourth."

"Excellent address," Jessie approved. "Now, if you can do something with the house…"

"If *you* can do something with the house," Max corrected her. "Decorating isn't my department."

"It isn't mine, either," Jessie said. "Actually, the job ought to be left for your wife. Most women like to have their own taste reflected in their homes."

"I guess," Max said, wondering what her apartment looked like. Jessie was such a decisive personality, she probably had the place decorated in bright jewel tones. He could almost see her lying on a ruby-red sofa. No, make that emerald green, he decided. Red would clash with her hair. Green would be a much better choice. It would highlight the almost translucent quality of her pale ivory skin.

"With an address like that, you should have a marvelous view of Central Park," she said.

"Here you are, sir." Fred pulled up in front of a five-story brownstone.

"You got a corner one," Jessie enthused. "You'll have light from three directions."

"I'll page you in about an hour, Fred," Max said as he got out of the car.

"Thanks, Fred," Jessie said as she scrambled after him, eager to view the house.

"It's really big." Jessie studied it from the sidewalk. "Are you sure this is the right one?" she asked, suddenly having the unnerving vision of walking in on some stranger.

Max held up the key, which had a small white tag attached. The address on the tag matched the number on the tarnished brass mailbox.

"Positive. Come on."

Jessie followed him across the sidewalk, peering into the half-basement windows. They had dirty-looking Venetian blinds on them, making it impossible to see inside.

She walked up the three stone steps to the impressive front door and examined the elaborate stained glass in the two long narrow windows that framed the door.

"Unless I miss my guess, those are Tiffany," she said.

"Tiffany?" Max frowned slightly as he inserted the key in the lock. "Didn't he do lamps?"

"Among other things. His studio was pretty prolific. Isn't it working?" She watched as he fiddled with the key.

"It's sticking. We may have to—" He broke off as the lock finally yielded. "First thing to take care of is having new locks installed," Max said as he shoved the door open.

Jessie wrinkled her nose as the odor of stale, musty house hit her. Hard on its heels came a stifling blast of hot air.

"Is there no air-conditioning, or is it just turned off?"

"I have no idea. What do you think?" Max asked as he looked around the spacious entryway.

"Well proportioned, and I'll bet that marble on the floor is original to the house."

"Don't worry about it. I can afford new."

"Don't you dare touch it!" Jessie said. "It's gorgeous. All it needs is to be cleaned and sealed."

"You think?" He studied the filthy floor uncertainly. There wasn't all that much contrast between the black and the white squares.

"Trust me. It'll be perfect."

Jessie walked through the archway on the right and found herself in a huge room with floor-to-ceiling windows on two walls. "Probably this was the main reception room," she said. "It looks too formal to be anything else. And I'll bet it's cold as the devil in the winter with all that glass."

Max walked over to one of the windows and poked at the sill. "It's rotted. Every window in the house will probably need to be replaced. Triple-paned glass should provide insulation as well as keep out the noise."

"Undoubtedly." Jessie pushed open the large double doors directly opposite the entrance to the reception room. The room was identical in size to the first room except that two of its walls were lined with bookshelves.

"The library?" Max guessed.

"Probably. Most houses this size and age had a library. Let's see what else is on this floor."

They found a dining room and three small rooms whose functions she wasn't sure of, as well as a bathroom with an old-fashioned toilet and pedestal sink.

"I was afraid of that," Jessie muttered.

"Afraid of what?" Max depressed the lever on the toilet and watched it flush. "It's old, but it seems to work."

"Not that. The kitchen," she said.

Max frowned as he mentally reviewed the rooms they'd inspected. "What kitchen?"

"My point exactly. There isn't one. I'll bet…"

Jessie walked over to the door at the end of the hallway. "This is probably the outside door," she said as she studied the chain on it.

"It's easy enough to check." Max stepped around her and unlocked it. It opened with a squeaking protest to reveal a yard surrounded by eight-foot-high red brick walls.

Jessie inched closer to him to see for herself and momentarily lost her focus when the spicy aroma of his cologne drifted into her lungs. He smells so sexy, she thought, as she surreptitiously took a second, deeper breath. So…

"Not a bad size for a city yard," Max observed, breaking into her thoughts.

With a monumental effort, Jessie forced herself to focus on what she was supposed to be doing with him and not on what she'd like to be doing.

"There's plenty of room to put in a big swing set and a playhouse. Once you get it cleaned up," she added when she noticed the glittering shards of broken glass lying on the ground.

Stepping back inside, she opened the door on the right and found herself staring into stygian blackness.

"All we need is a body," she muttered.

"Or lights," Max said dryly, as he reached around her and turned the switch beside the door.

A single feeble light flickered to life in the stairwell.

Jessie grimaced. "I didn't realize they made lightbulbs that dim," she said as she cautiously started down the stairs.

At the bottom she found herself in a hallway that ran the length of the house and had six doors in it. She opened each door and stuck her head into empty dusty rooms. The last one revealed a kitchen.

"I rented an apartment once that had a kitchen like this," Max said thoughtfully as he studied the twenties-era appliances. "But why is the kitchen down here?"

"Because this is the way a lot of these old mansions were built. The kitchens were on the basement level, and the food was sent up in a dumbwaiter. The other rooms were probably servants' quarters."

"Sounds like they ate a lot of cold food." Max wandered over to the stove and pulled open the oven door. It gave a creaking groan and came off in his hand.

Jessie chuckled at his surprised expression. "I wouldn't touch anything down here."

"Now she tells me." Max dropped the oven door on the floor and said, "Let's get out of here. This level is hopeless." He moved aside so she could go up the stairs first.

The delicate scent of her floral perfume teased his nostrils as she walked past him. He took a deep breath and started coughing when he inhaled a lungful of dust.

"You okay?" Jessie demanded once they were back on the first floor.

"Yes, it's just dusty down there."

Jessie glanced around the empty hall, her eyes lingering on the pile of dead leaves in the corner. "It's dusty everywhere. I wonder how those leaves got in here."

Max shrugged. "Don't know and don't care, as long as they get out. Let's finish this before one of us succumbs to an asthma attack."

"Do you have asthma?" Jessie asked nervously.

"No, but this place would be enough to induce it." He kicked aside the pile of debris at the bottom of a graceful staircase.

"The staircase is gorgeous," Jessie said. "It looks to be mahogany."

"Some of the rails are missing."

"They can be duplicated and replaced." Jessie headed up the stairs.

"Why bother? It would be easier to just replace the whole thing."

"Easier and probably cheaper than restoring it, but trust me, it wouldn't be anywhere near as effective. Having a period house that has been faithfully restored will be a plus with your future wife. At least, it should be, if she comes from the society crowd." Jessie qualified her statement.

"I'm not putting up with cold food and antique plumbing to keep anyone happy, and that includes a wife," Max said flatly.

"Restored within limits." Jessie amended her statement. "If you were to knock those three rooms that don't seem to have any function together, you could install a state-of-the-art kitchen on the first floor along with a family room off it."

"What should be done with the basement?" Max asked, impressed with how quickly she came up with ideas.

"A laundry room, an exercise room and a huge playroom for the kids."

Max followed her back upstairs as he considered her words. He could easily visualize his kids running around the large, open space. There were two little boys with his dark hair chasing a small girl with bright-red curly hair and... He hastily cut off the thought. His daughter would probably have blond hair because his wife would probably be a blonde. He always dated blondes.

"This floor is going to need extensive remodeling, too." Jessie voice came from slightly ahead of him.

He hurried after her as she disappeared inside one of the open doorways on the second floor and found himself standing in a good-size room with five windows alongside one wall.

"Lots of natural light," he said.

"Uh-huh, and no closets." She walked through the open door in the opposite wall. "Interesting, there's a connecting door to the next room."

"They didn't seem to be much on privacy, did they?" Max said.

"No, but if you knocked out the wall between these two rooms you could have one big bedroom with a large dressing room and an up-to-date bath."

"I'm beginning to think that the house'll have to be gutted to the outside walls," Max said.

"You could be right." Jessie walked over to a pile of plaster on the floor and then looked up. The ceiling had collapsed at some point, and she had a clear view of the room above.

Max followed her gaze. "Forget going up there," he said. "It doesn't look any too safe. I'll get hold of an architect today."

"I suggest calling Leaverson and Leaverson," Jessie said. "They specialize in restoring old brownstones, and they do a marvelous job."

They weren't the only ones who did a marvelous job, Max thought as he studied her thoughtful features. Hiring Jessie Martinelli was turning out to be one of the best ideas he'd had in years.

Chapter Four

"What does your schedule look like for the rest of the week?" Max asked once they were back in the car.

Jessie mentally checked her calendar and then said, "I have an afternoon meeting on Thursday. Summers tend to be slow because most companies are reluctant to schedule workshops with so many people out on vacation."

"What's the event on Thursday?"

"I'm meeting with a headmaster to discuss giving a lesson on table manners at his school this fall."

"A school?" Max looked surprised. "I didn't realize schools did etiquette."

"Most don't. This one is a very forward-thinking private school. According to the headmaster, the parents are worried about the lack of manners in their offspring and have demanded the school do something about it."

"And he agreed?" Max asked.

"When you're charging parents twenty-five thousand a

year you tend to be very responsive to said parents' demands," Jessie said dryly. "You'll find out in a few years. It's the kind of place your kids will go to. Very exclusive with a waiting list a mile long. I believe the theory is that sending your kids there will ensure that they grow up knowing the people who will become the movers and shakers on the New York business scene."

Max frowned at her tart tone. "You don't agree with the theory?"

Jessie shrugged. "I'm in business. Every businesswoman knows the value of contacts."

"But?" Max persisted.

"But as a person, I think we ought to let kids be kids and not limit their friends to those who might do them some financial good in the future."

"At least they have parents who care enough to make the effort to provide the best background they can," Max countered.

"I think it might be more accurate to say they have parents who have the money to pay others to make the effort. There's nothing I'm going to teach these kids that they couldn't learn by eating meals with their parents. But their parents are so busy with either making money or enjoying themselves that their kids are being raised by a series of nannies and au pairs."

"Ignoring your offspring isn't just a trait of the wealthy and socially prominent," Max argued from the bitter depths of his own memories.

"No, it isn't," Jessie said flatly.

Max wondered at the pain he could see in her green eyes. Had his words triggered bad memories for her? And if so, were they personal memories, or could she be thinking about those kids at the center last night?

"What kind of childhood did you have?" he asked.

"Par for the course," Jessie said, soothing her conscience by telling herself that she wasn't really lying. Her childhood had been par for the course for a kid whose mother had been an alcoholic prostitute. It wasn't her fault if Max jumped to a wrong conclusion and assumed she came from a normal, middle-class background.

"We need to get you started on tennis lessons as soon as possible," she said, determinedly changing the subject. "I'll call my tennis club and see if they have a free court this afternoon."

"I've been thinking about that…" he began.

"Sounds more like you've been thinking about ways to weasel out of the lessons. When you hire an expert, you should listen to the expert. And your expert is telling you that a working knowledge of tennis is essential. Although…"

She eyed him thoughtfully for a long moment.

"I don't like what you're thinking," he said dryly.

"You don't know what I'm thinking."

"Anyone with an ounce of self-preservation can recognize the gleam in your eyes as trouble."

"I was simply trying to come up with a scenario to explain why you don't play tennis or sail," Jessie said slowly.

"And?" he asked, curious about how her mind worked.

"We could always claim you have a chronic inner ear problem that affects your sense of balance. That would explain all kinds of failings," she added, warming to the idea. "Even being clumsy on the dance floor."

"No," Max said flatly. "I refuse to paint myself as pathetic. Pity is worse than outright enmity."

Jessie shrugged. "Then you're stuck with the lessons."

Max stared out the window as he considered her words. She was right. It would be stupid of him to ignore her advice simply because he found tennis monumentally boring. He could put up with short-term boredom in order to further his long-term goals.

"All right. I'll learn tennis, but we'll use my health club. They have courts."

Unhooking his cell phone from his belt, he opened it and dialed.

"Al, this is Max Sheridan. Can I get a tennis court this afternoon? Just a second, I'll check," he said after a moment.

"He says he has a cancellation at three o'clock. Does that work for you?"

Jessie nodded.

"Three's fine, Al. One hour should be more than enough time. Thanks." Max hung up.

An hour should be about right, Jessie thought. She didn't want to overdo it at first. Although...

Uncertainly she stared at his broad chest.

"What's wrong?"

"Tennis is a rather strenuous sport," she said slowly. "What kind of shape are you in?"

"Good," he said.

Actually, he looked to be in spectacular shape, she thought wryly, but looks could be very deceptive, and one read in the papers all the time about high-powered businessmen in their thirties and forties dropping dead of a heart attack. Fear momentarily iced her skin, and she shivered at the thought of all that vitality of Max's suddenly snuffed out.

"Is that assessment yours or someone who counts?" she persisted.

Max looked down his nose at her. "And my opinion doesn't count?"

"People are rarely objective about their own health,"

Jessie said as memories of her mother's lifelong denial of her alcoholism floated through her mind.

"According to my doctor, who gave me my annual physical last month, I'm in perfect health," Max said. "Don't worry. You won't have to practice your CPR on me."

"Why do you think I know CPR?"

He grinned, and her mouth dried as the charm in his unexpected smile washed over her.

"You're the type to be prepared."

He made her sound like a cross between a Boy Scout and Pollyanna, Jessie thought in annoyance. Why couldn't he have looked at her and seen... Seen what? She mocked her thoughts. She'd seen pictures of some of his former girlfriends and the only thing she had in common with them was her sex. Besides, his lack of interest in her as a woman was safer. Much safer. Getting involved with Max Sheridan would be a one-way ticket to disaster, because there was no way she could ever fit into his plans on anything other than a temporary basis.

"How about if I drop you off at your apartment so you can pick up some tennis clothes and a swimsuit while I run over to my office. I'll pick you back up at two-thirty."

"It's twelve-fifteen."

Max frowned at her. "What's that got to do with anything?"

"Doesn't your staff eat lunch?"

"After that SOS Pearsall sent me, he'd better be eating at his desk until I arrive or he can eat all his meals elsewhere," Max said flatly.

Jessie shivered at his implacable tone, and she suddenly had no trouble at all believing that this man had built a business empire with his bare hands. He brought whole new shades of meaning to the term *single-minded*.

"Two-thirty's fine, and I won't need a swimsuit since I have no intention of going anywhere near a pool."

"Oh, yes, you are," Max contradicted her. "Fred and I both told you that knowing how to swim is essential, and my health club has a big pool. That's why we're using my club instead of yours."

"You're missing the salient point here, Max," Jessie said doggedly, having the odd feeling that she was standing in the middle of a freeway trying to dodge the oncoming traffic. "I don't want to learn how to swim."

"And I don't want to learn how to play tennis. Think of it as a trade-off."

"There are so many fallacies in that argument I don't know where to begin. Besides, I don't own a swimsuit," she said, telling herself it wasn't really a lie. The suits she owned hadn't been designed for swimming, just sitting around in the sun.

"No problem, my club's shop sells swimsuits."

"Undoubtedly overpriced. I have better things to do with my money."

"If you'll remember, I told you that I would be responsible for any clothes you needed to buy. A swimsuit comes under that heading. And while we're on the subject, you'll need to get something for the Biddles' cocktail party."

"I have clothes I can wear," Jessie said.

"Humor me," he said. "Buy something new. A designer model. As you keep telling me, you only get one chance to make a first impression."

Maybe she should take advantage of his offer and get a designer gown. An original model would make sure she fit in, and fitting in was the first step to doing business with people like the Biddles.

"While I'm in the office, I'll have accounting issue you

a company credit card so you don't have to use your own," Max said as Fred double-parked in front of her apartment building. "And check with me before you take on any more commitments, because I intend to keep you busy. I'll call Leaverson to set up a meeting to go over the house and tell me what's feasible. I want you along to give me a woman's view."

Jessie savored the spurt of pleasure she felt at being part of bringing the old house back to life and forced herself to say, "The woman whose opinion you need is your future wife."

"I haven't got one at the moment, and I don't want to delay getting started on the remodeling. There's too much that needs to be done."

"There is that," Jessie conceded. "I guess it won't hurt. I mean, you'll mostly be guided by the architect's ideas and what the basic structure of the house will allow."

"Right. I'll be back for you at two-thirty."

"Bye." Jessie threw the word somewhere between the already preoccupied Max and the silently watchful Fred and hastily got out of the car. Clearly Max had already switched mental gears and was in his business-tycoon role. A smile curved her lips as she watched the car pull away. Max really was the most fascinating individual. She'd never met anyone anywhere nearly as focused as he was.

She grimaced as she let herself into her apartment building. Or anyone as determined to get his own way. It looked as if she was going to put up with yet one more person trying to teach her to swim.

The first thing she noticed when she opened her apartment door was the blinking light on her answering machine. Dropping her purse on the floor, she walked over and pushed the play button. The first two messages were business, and she carefully jotted the call-back numbers on the notepad beside the phone.

Her mood of satisfaction was abruptly shattered when the third message began to play. She shuddered, and her stomach twisted painfully at the sound of a voice she hadn't heard in fifteen years.

"Jessie, I know this is probably too soon after my letter, but—"

Jessie reached out a shaking hand and jabbed the erase button. The sudden silence was almost as overpowering as the unexpected voice had been.

She clenched her hands into fists in a vain attempt to stop their trembling, and sank down on the couch as she fought to steady her ragged breathing.

"Why?" she muttered in angry confusion. Why was her mother suddenly so eager to see her? It had been fifteen long years since that awful Saturday when she'd woken to find their two-room apartment full of cops who had been busily handcuffing her mother. As usual, her mother had been drunk.

Jessie had been told to get dressed, and then the police had taken her and her mother down to the station. Her mother had disappeared behind a dingy steel door, and Jessie had been handed over to a harried social worker, who'd bundled the petrified Jessie into a car and driven out to Long Island, where she'd left her at a temporary foster home with the parting advice to behave herself and everything would be fine.

"Damn!" Jessie jumped to her feet, too agitated to sit still, and headed for the kitchen to make herself a cup of coffee. She didn't want to remember that time in her life. Didn't want to remember the pain and the terrifying fear of being at the mercy of people she didn't know and forces she couldn't understand. Nor did she want to remember her mother, who had caused it all to happen.

Jessie turned the gas on under the kettle and took a jar of instant espresso out of the cabinet.

Her hand shook as she spooned the granules into a cup, and she spilled some on the counter. She didn't even notice. She was too caught up in old memories and new fears.

It wasn't that she wished her mother ill, she assured herself. She hoped that she was a bigger person than that. It was just that she didn't want anything to do with her. Her mother had made her choices long ago, and those choices had left Jessie out in the cold. Whatever it was in a person that inspired love and commitment from another, Jessie didn't have. She'd faced that unpalatable fact years ago when her mother hadn't loved her enough to provide even a minimum level of care.

Hastily Jessie cut off the line of thought. No good ever came from brooding over what couldn't be changed.

The water started to boil, and Jessie poured it into the cup with an unsteady hand. All she had to do was to refuse any contact with her mother, and everything would be okay, she told herself. In a couple of days her mother would lose interest and move on to other things, just as she always had.

Blindly Jessie groped for the coffee cup and took a sip of the caffeine-laden brew. Or she'd get drunk and forget that she'd ever had a daughter. The only constant from her childhood had been her mother's drinking. Her excessive drinking. She very much doubted that fifteen years would have changed that.

But she had changed. She wasn't a child anymore. She was an adult. An adult who knew better than to believe in fairy tales and empty promises. An adult who'd faced her limitations and made her peace with the fact that a husband

and children was something she could never have. She'd
learned to be happy with what she could have—a thriving
business and her volunteer work at the center.

An image of Max formed in her mind, and a comforting feeling of warmth sparked to life deep inside her,
spreading outward to warm her icy skin. He really was the
most fascinating man. Totally unlike anyone she had ever
met. And his appeal had nothing to do with the indecent
amount of money he had. It was… She struggled to understand her fascination with him.

It was his intensity, she finally decided. Max Sheridan
was the most intense man she'd ever met. He seemed to
radiate a force field that brought the people around him to
tingling life. When she was with Max her world seemed
sharper, clearer. And infinitely more dangerous, she conceded. Her mind might know for an absolute fact that
falling for Max would be the height of stupidity, but her
emotions were oblivious to that reality.

The wife he was determined to acquire would have to
be careful not to expect too much from him, Jessie thought,
because it was becoming increasingly clear to her that a
wife would never occupy center stage in Max's life. That
position was reserved for business. A woman would always
come in a poor second or even third behind his kids.

Maybe Max was simply being sensible to pick a wife
with his head and not his heart. From what she'd observed,
a marriage founded on love took a lot of work to make it
a success, whereas a relationship where each person went
into it with no illusions should be relatively easy to make
a success of. If one could call a marriage that only skated
on the surface of one's emotions a success.

In some ways she and Max had a lot in common. If the
newspaper accounts of his early life were accurate, they

had both had miserable childhoods. Each had had to make their own way in the world without help from anyone else. But instead of their similar backgrounds forming a bond between them, it only served to drive a wedge between them because Max was determined to expunge the past.

Although in a way, she'd done the same thing. Jessie stared blindly at the oversize clock on the wall. It could be argued that she'd set up her adult life to be the antithesis of her childhood. Where her mother had surrounded herself with emotional, financial and legal chaos, Jessie strove for order and security. Her house was always immaculate. Nothing was ever out of place. She kept meticulous financial records. She had a healthy investment portfolio, and the only debt she carried was the mortgage on her co-op. Not only that but she was so leery of the law she deliberately overpaid her taxes, just to be on the safe side. And while her mother had leaped into relationships with no thought as to the danger she was courting, Jessie was very, very cautious about risking emotional involvement.

Both she and Max had been scarred by their upbringings, not that the past seemed to be slowing Max down any. She grimaced. She doubted that a fully loaded freight train would slow him down.

Maybe Max had been right. Maybe she ought to consider a marriage like the one he was setting up. Jessie took another sip of coffee as she weighed the idea. She already knew she didn't have what it took to inspire long-term emotional commitment from anyone. But if she wasn't looking for any depth of emotion in her marriage or any children… If she were only looking for companionship…

Jessie frowned. It might work. But it might also lead to disaster, she conceded.

No, her original plan to stay single and heart-whole was the much better idea. That way she could stay in control.

Taking her coffee, she went into the living room to switch on the computer, intending to fill the time until Max returned with work.

At two twenty-eight she was standing in the lobby of her apartment building waiting for Max. She didn't wait long. The big Mercedes pulled up at precisely two-thirty. Jessie pushed open the lobby door and walked toward the car, wondering how Fred managed to arrive everywhere exactly on time. She would have thought that the traffic, if nothing else, would make him late occasionally.

The car's back door opened, and Max stepped out. Jessie's breath caught in her lungs as the bright sunshine splintered off his dark head. He looked absolutely gorgeous.

Max took the gym bag and tennis rackets she was carrying and stood aside for her to enter the car.

"Good afternoon." She tried her best to sound professionally cheerful. "I brought along a spare tennis racket for you."

"I thought I'd pick one up at the club while you got a swimsuit. They sell everything there."

"Good, then I want to buy a refusal so you'll believe me when I say I don't want to learn to swim."

"I won't have your death on my conscience," Max said. "You will learn to swim."

"Tell me, do you have much luck with the forceful approach?" she asked dryly.

Max grinned at her, and her stomach did a quick flip-flop.

"People who work for me tend to take orders well. Or they don't continue to work for me."

"Is that a threat?" she demanded.

"Try considering it a friendly warning."

Jessie pressed her lips together in annoyance, wondering why it was so important to him that he teach her to swim. Unless… Could it be a guy thing? Max was used to being the one in charge. The one with all the answers. Could he subconsciously resent the fact that in their relationship she was the expert and he was the student?

Surreptitiously she studied his profile, her gaze lingering on the firm line of his chin. It was possible. Maybe his teaching her to swim in some way evened the scales a little in his eyes.

"You don't understand," she finally said. "I have had swimming lessons before. They didn't take."

"How so?"

Jessie grimaced. "The unvarnished truth is I almost drowned in the school pool when I was in seventh grade and I'm…"

"Scared of the water?" he finished for her.

"Petrified would be more accurate."

"And you never tried to get over it?" he asked incredulously. "Your parents didn't insist on it?"

Jessie swallowed a bitter comment. When the school had tried to get in contact with her mother to tell her what had happened and to ask her to meet them at the hospital's emergency room, they hadn't been able to reach her. Her mother had been down at the local bar getting drunk as usual. And as for her father…Jessie had no idea who her father was. And neither, she suspected, did her mother. But that was not the kind of information one gave to a client. Or to anyone else, for that matter.

"No, my parents didn't insist on it."

"They should have," he said. "What happens when you have kids of your own? Are you going to pass along your fear of water to them?"

Kids of her own? Jessie considered his words, and her mind obligingly supplied a picture of a dark-haired little boy with Max's eyes and engaging grin. Hastily she wiped the image. What was the matter with her? she wondered uneasily. She'd never fantasized about having munchkins before. So why was being around Max making her think about kids? Maybe because the whole reason for their relationship was so that he could marry and have a family?

"Jessie?" His deep voice cut into her confused thoughts, and she realized the car had stopped. She looked out the window to find they were in front of a health club. A far fancier place than the small, rather shabby tennis club she belonged to.

"It looks very nice," she said. "Although I would have expected someone with your financial resources to have their own gym."

"I'm not and never have been into conspicuous consumption. Besides, having other people working out around me provides an incentive for me to keep going. And quit changing the subject. You have to learn to swim!"

Jessie gave him a disgruntled look. "Tell me. Are you a fan of Chinese water torture?"

"Do you view repeating the truth as torture?" he retorted.

Jessie shook her head as she got out of the car. "I'll make you a deal. I'll give learning to swim a shot, but if I panic you agree to drop the whole thing."

"For today," he agreed, and Jessie couldn't decide whether to be annoyed at his incredible persistence or to admire it. One thing was certain. Max Sheridan was rather like an onrushing avalanche. Nothing stopped him. He simply swept everything out of his path.

Max ushered her into the health club, past a doorman

who looked like he competed in weight-lifting contests in his spare time and into the pro shop.

He headed toward the racks of swimsuits and stopped in front of a selection of minuscule bikinis. Picking up a black one, he held it out to her. "What about this one?"

Jessie eyed the tiny scraps of lycra dangling between his long fingers and felt heat engulf her at the thought of wearing something so revealing around him. Not that he'd be likely to notice, she thought. If his past girlfriends were any indication, he wouldn't even glance at someone built as slightly as she was.

Which was good, she assured herself. She certainly didn't want him to think of her as anything other than a colleague.

"Not my style," she said, and moved toward the Speedo swimsuit rack behind him. "I'll have one of these." She rummaged through them and pulled out a royal-blue one in a size six.

Jessie didn't object when he told the sales clerk to put the swimsuit on his bill. She saw no reason to spend her own money to buy something she most emphatically didn't want.

Max handed her the plastic bag with the swimsuit and then glanced at his watch. "It's about time for our court reservation. I'll show you where the locker rooms are, and you can get changed."

The locker rooms were more luxurious than her living room, and Jessie wondered what a membership in this place cost. Probably more a month than her mortgage payment, she thought with a faintly envious sigh as she hurriedly changed into her tennis clothes.

She found Max waiting for her just outside the women's locker room doors, and her mouth dried as she studied him. He looked spectacular in white shorts and polo shirt. His long, heavily muscled legs were lightly covered with dark hair that made her fingers itch with the desire to touch. What on earth was the matter with her? she wondered uneasily. She'd never noticed a man's legs before. Legs were just there. So what was different about Max's? She had no idea, so she tried her best to ignore her atypical reaction. It wasn't easy.

"Where are the tennis courts?" Jessie asked.

"On the basement level. Come on." He led the way to the elevator and punched the down button. A second later the silver doors parted with a ding.

"Why, hello there, Max." A bright, chirpy voice from the back of the elevator greeted them as they entered.

Jessie blinked as she got a good look at the gorgeous brunette dressed in a pair of spandex shorts and a tight T-shirt.

"We met the other day in the weight room." The woman gave Max a megawatt white smile that the American Dental Association could have used on a poster.

Max merely nodded and then turned to Jessie, effectively cutting the woman off.

Despite knowing that it was small-minded of her, Jessie couldn't help the surge of pleasure his seeming indifference to the beautiful brunette gave her.

The elevator came to a dignified stop on the ground floor, and Max shepherded Jessie toward the tennis courts. Like everything else in the building they were well designed and in perfect repair.

"By the way, we have an appointment with Leaverson on Monday to go over the house."

Jessie blinked. "How did you manage such a quick one?"

Max shrugged. "I asked."

And they probably recognized his name, Jessie thought. Doing Max Sheridan's house would undoubtedly bring Leaverson a lot of referral business. Not only that, but Max wouldn't argue about the cost or try to cut corners on quality. From what she'd seen, he was not tight with his money like so many of the wealthy she'd dealt with.

"Monday's fine," Jessie said. "Now, for your tennis lesson. I think all we'll worry about today is getting you comfortable lobbing the ball back and forth over the net. You can study the rules of the game in your spare time." She frowned. "I should have checked to see if they had a book on how to play tennis in the pro shop."

"I'll have my P.A. order one from the bookstore," Max said. "Which side of the court do I get?"

"You stay on this side, I'll take the other."

Jessie trotted around the net and walked to the far baseline. She took a couple of bright-yellow balls out of her can before rolling it to the back wall out of the way. Gently she lobbed one a ball over to him. It came back so fast she blinked.

Jessie studied Max for a long second. So he wanted to play rough, did he? She gave him a slow smile that would have had anyone who knew her backing away in a hurry. She might be a woman and not have his upper-body strength, but she hadn't lost any of the skills that had made her nationally ranked in the NCAA during her college years.

"Did I hit it too hard?" Max gave her an innocent smile that she instinctively mistrusted. He could do with a lesson on the dangers of underestimating people, and she was just the one to give it to him.

"No problem. I just wasn't paying attention. I'll do better. Are you ready?"

"Sure."

Jessie served with her normal speed, skillfully placing the ball where he had to scramble to reach it. His return went wild.

"The goal is to return the ball between the lines," she said as she slammed another serve across the net.

Max managed to get his racket on the ball this time, but it didn't clear the net.

Five minutes later, when he hadn't been able to return a single one of her serves, he walked over to the net and waited.

Warily Jessie approached him, wondering what kind of reaction she was going to get. She already knew he was the quintessential competitor; what she was about to find out was what kind of loser he was.

"This is because I hit the ball too hard the first time, isn't it?" He came right to the point.

"I thought 'no holds barred' was the way you wanted to play it," Jessie said.

Max gave her a long, thoughtful look. "The hell you did. You're trying to teach me a lesson, and you're good enough to do it. You're very much like me, when all is said and done."

Jessie frowned, not following his train of thought. "How so?"

"You're as competitive as hell."

"Only about some things. Would you prefer to simply practice lobbing the ball back and forth?" she asked.

"Of course I would. I'm not stupid. At least, not serially stupid." Max gave her a rueful smile.

Satisfied that she now had him in a mind-set where he could learn something, she settled down into getting him familiar with hitting the ball.

Max concentrated on returning her lobs with a single-mindedness that she suspected he normally applied only to making money. Or did he apply that same concentration to everything he was learning? she wondered. A flush burned over her cheeks at the thought of him setting out to learn what pleased a woman in bed.

Jessie was so wrapped up in her thoughts that she failed to notice when a ball escaped from the court next to theirs and rolled under her feet. She tripped over it and landed painfully on her leg.

"Jessie!" Max vaulted the net and hurried over to her.

Despite being impressed by his leap, she said, "Next time go around the net. That's a good way to break your neck and other assorted body parts." And breaking anything on his magnificent body would be a real shame, she thought as she started to get up.

"Don't move," Max commanded. "You might have injured yourself."

"No, the only injury done was to my dignity." She tried not to react to the intoxicating feel of his hands moving over the bare skin of her leg, presumably checking for breaks.

"Your knee is bleeding!" He sounded outraged, but at what she wasn't sure.

"It's just oozing. I'll put an antiseptic on it and it'll be fine."

Max scowled at the raw-looking skin on her knee.

"You need to see a doctor."

"Hardly. Although I certainly can't go into a pool." She suddenly realized that there was a silver lining to her accident.

"Don't think I'm going to forget about teaching you to swim."

"When my knee is healed," Jessie said as she hobbled off the court, wondering how long she could milk this injury. With luck, at least a week.

She absolutely had to get a grip. She was acting like a teenager in the throes of a crush, and not like the professional she knew herself to be.

Chapter Five

Jessie glanced up the street, looking for Max's Mercedes, and when she didn't see it she went back to studying her reflection in the glass doors of her apartment building. A deep sense of satisfaction filled her as she studied her new cocktail dress. It was gorgeous, even if she did say so herself. At least, what there was of it was gorgeous. She glanced down at the plunging neckline, which exposed the top third of her breasts. It was the most daring thing she had ever worn. And by far the most expensive.

She squashed the flash of guilt she felt at the memory of just how expensive the dress had actually been. Max was right. She needed to fit in if she was to have any hope of overhearing conversations between other women in the ladies' room. And the easiest way to fit in was to look like everyone else in the room and that meant she had to wear a designer dress. And for designer read expensive.

Jessie grimaced as she moved slightly, and her skinned

knee twinged. She was not looking forward to the Biddles' party. She hated the kinds of events where overdressed, overprivileged, smugly self-satisfied people mingled with others of their ilk and discussed such riveting topics as the difficulty of finding a good nanny. If she could have risked having children, she wouldn't have turned them over to a nanny to raise. She'd keep them close. As close as she could. She'd…she'd probably warp them as badly as her mother had warped her, because she didn't even know enough about parenting to know what would damage a child and what wouldn't. And the world didn't need any more damaged souls.

Determinedly she banished all thoughts of kids and forced herself to concentrate on what she was supposed to be doing for Max. Somehow she couldn't see Max thriving in that kind of insular environment. He was far too vibrant. Too down-to-earth. From what she'd seen, he didn't have a pretentious bone in his body. She couldn't see him exchanging the same boring platitudes with the same boring people for the rest of his life.

But then, what did she really know about Max? she reminded herself. It would be a big mistake for her to assume that she understood him just because she enjoyed his company. For all she knew he could find her every bit as boring as she found people like the Biddles. And he could be hiding his boredom because he was basically a kind man. His hiring Luis was proof of that.

Hurriedly, she pushed open the lobby door as Max's Mercedes pulled up. His getting a ticket for double-parking would not be a good way to start the evening. She had the feeling it was going to be stressful enough without that.

Max stepped out of the car and then froze as he caught sight of Jessie emerging from her apartment building. Her fiery red hair had been artfully arranged in a cascade of curls that spilled down her neck.

His eyes traced the garment from its plunging neckline down over her slender body to where it ended at her knees. His eyes continued their downward path over her delicate ankles to focus on the fragile black strappy four-inch heels she was wearing. The shoes made her small feet look even smaller and seemed to lengthen her slender legs.

Jessie blinked at the sight of Max's broad frame encased in a perfectly tailored black suit. James Bond in any of his incarnations hadn't looked half as good as Max did, she thought. And it was a bad sign that she was responding to him the same way she did to a box of hand-dipped chocolate creams. With the urge to dive right in and gorge herself, giving no thought to the long-term consequences.

"Hi," she said, praying that the excitement that gripped her wasn't visible in her face. It would be humiliating in the extreme if he were to realize that she was attracted to him.

"Good evening, Fred," Jessie said as she gracefully slipped into the car.

"Evening, Ms. Martinelli." Fred never took his eyes off the street.

Max got in beside her, and Jessie tensed as the warmth of his large body crowded her. This close she could smell the tantalizing citrusy tang of his cologne, and it was doing odd things to her equilibrium. Trying to make the move appear casual, Jessie inched closer to the opposite window in an attempt to put a little distance between her and the source of her temptation. The added inches didn't help a bit.

Max's eyes narrowed as he caught a glimpse of her black-nylon-covered thigh. "Aren't those hose bothering your injured knee?"

"Not all that much." She made an effort to introduce a neutral subject. "It's surprisingly cool for July."

"What about your shoes?" Max went on, fixing his gaze on her feet. He'd never paid much attention to a woman's feet before, but Jessie's were well worth a second look. Her delicate ankles and high arches were highlighted by the fragility of her shoes.

"What about my shoes?" Jessie glanced down at them in confusion. "I don't like the turn this conversation has taken," Jessie said. "Let's talk about something else."

"What else?"

"How about the background to this affair we're going to? How well do you know the Biddles?"

"I've done business with his bank for years."

"Is this the first time you've socialized with him?"

"I had a working dinner with him and four other businessmen once. This is the first time I've been to his home."

"Why did he invite you?" Jessie asked.

"You don't think it was for my charming personality?" Max asked dryly.

"From what I've heard about Edwin Biddle, he never does anything without a reason—a self-serving reason. If he's suddenly added you to his guest list, it's because he wants something."

Max's features hardened, and a nervous shiver chased down her spine at his implacable expression. Max would make a truly terrifying enemy.

"Simply because he wants something doesn't mean I intend to give it to him."

"I guess not," Jessie said, reminding herself that Max was not some naive country boy who needed protecting. He'd come a long way since he'd left rural Georgia. But even so, being able to win in the business arena did not necessarily mean he could win at the kinds of social games the inhabitants of the Biddles' world played.

"Are you worried about me, Jessie?" Max asked curiously. He'd never in his life had anyone worry about him. Not even his parents. Especially not his parents.

"I'm responsible for you, in a way," Jessie said slowly. "Besides, I need to keep you out of trouble long enough for you to find a suitable wife."

"You shouldn't have any problems. I've never been the impulsive type, and I know exactly what I want."

Jessie eyed him across the darkened car, her eyes lingering on the enticing line of his firm lips. She wished she could be as sure about what she wanted, she thought. No, that wasn't true. She knew what she wanted. She wanted to kiss Max Sheridan. She wanted to grab him and tumble him down onto the nearest bed and make mad, passionate love to him. And she really wished she knew why she would want to do anything so self-destructive as to get involved with a client. Even knowing that Max didn't feel anything for her or that he never would, she still wanted to make love to him. Which said what about her common sense? she wondered uneasily.

Max glanced over at Jessie. She looked so alone. So inexplicably sad that he wanted to gather her in his arms and hold her close. To protect her, despite the fact that he knew she didn't need his protection. Jessie Martinelli was a highly paid professional doing a job she was well qualified to do. The expression on her face was undoubtedly a trick of the light. Her emotions weren't involved.

He scowled. Unlike his own, which were bouncing all over the place. Now that he was finally putting his plan into action it was hardly surprising that he would be a little nervous, he reassured himself. He might well be meeting his future wife tonight. The mother of his children. The woman he was going to trust enough to let her raise his kids. Which reminded him…

"I'll have to talk to my lawyer about a prenup," he said.

"What?" Jessie said, not following his abrupt change of subject.

"I said I'll have to see my lawyer about drawing up a prenup."

Jessie frowned at him. "I would strongly suggest that you hold off on any talk of a prenup until after you've proposed. Most women would find it very disquieting to have the guy making plans for the divorce before they've even made it to the altar."

"I try to be totally honest in personal relationships, and the truth is that while I am perfectly willing to indulge my wife's taste for luxury as long as she remains married to me, I have no intention of providing a fortune for her to set up on her own. I want that understood up front."

Any woman lucky enough to get Max to the altar would have to be out of her mind to divorce him, Jessie thought. He had everything any woman could possibly want in a man. Except maybe trust. Max was definitely short on trust.

"By the way," Max said, "I meant to tell you that your protégé bombed out of the mailroom today."

"My protégé?" Jessie blinked, scrambling to drag her thoughts away from Max. It wasn't easy. Her mind felt as if it was wading through honey.

"Luis," Max said.

"What was Luis doing in the mailroom?" she asked.

"Human Resources thought it would be a harmless place to shove someone without any of the normal skills."

Jessie winced at Max's sardonic expression. "I take it they were wrong?"

"Considering that Luis doesn't appear to be able to read... Or did you already know that?"

Jessie sighed. "No. I would have tried to do something about it if I had. I don't really know Luis all that well. I mostly deal with the preteens."

Max studied Jessie's worried features in exasperation. "Tell me, do you feel responsible for correcting all the world's ills?"

"Nope, just the ones in my little corner of it. So what happened?"

"Instead of just admitting that he couldn't read to whom the mail was addressed, he had a stab at delivering it. We're going to be chasing some of it down for days!"

"That was your fault," Jessie insisted.

"Mine!"

"Yes, yours," she insisted. "You were the one who told him to go with half lies."

Max opened his mouth and then closed it when fairness made him admit there might be something in what she said.

"That wasn't what I meant, and you know it," he finally said.

"I may know it, and you may know it, but how would you expect a seventeen-year-old with no business experience to know it? There has to be something he can do?"

"What odds will you give me?" Max said dryly.

"Did you fire him?"

"No. I told him to find out where the nearest adult literacy center is and get himself enrolled, and then I told him to figure out what he thinks he could do, and we'd discuss it."

Jessie breathed a sigh of relief that Luis still had a chance.

"Thanks for not firing him out of hand," Jessie said.

"Thanks are premature. The jury's still out on his final fate."

"Here we are, sir," Fred announced.

Jessie glanced out the car window to find herself in front of a four-story brownstone that spilled light from all its front windows.

"It's not as big as mine, and it's not on a corner," Max said with satisfaction.

"Comparisons are odious," Jessie said repressively as she climbed out of the car. "And if that doesn't stop you, try concentrating on the *condition* of your bigger town house."

Max climbed out after her. "Only temporarily. After Leaverson sees it, things should move pretty quickly."

"Hopefully. Although it would probably help if you bring a portfolio of pictures to show to Leaverson that illustrate your ideas of what you want the finished house to look like," she said.

"I don't have any ideas."

"Get some," Jessie said.

"Where?"

"Building and decorating magazines would be a good place to start looking, or think about houses you've visited and what you liked about them."

"Any last-minute advice before we ring up the curtain on this performance?" Max asked.

"Performance" was right, Jessie thought. She felt as if she was taking part in an elaborate costume play. All that remained to be seen whether it was a drama or a farce.

"No advice. This evening definitely comes under the heading of if 'twere done, 'twere best done quickly," Jessie muttered.

Max frowned slightly. "Wasn't that quote in reference to a murder?" he asked as he pushed the bell beside the door.

Jessie was spared having to admit that she wasn't sure when the door opened to reveal a butler in a morning coat.

Pretentious, Jessie thought as the majestic-looking man stepped aside for them to enter. A maid to open the door would have been sufficient.

Once they were inside, Jessie surreptitiously looked around the spacious hallway, noting the antique French bombé chest with an enormous arrangement of fresh flowers on it. What looked like an antique oriental rug in shades of reddish brown covered the cream marble floor.

The place fairly reeked of old money.

Max instinctively moved closer to her as he noticed some guy at the end of the hall eyeing her as if she were a juicy steak and he hadn't had a square meal in weeks.

"The next time you go shopping I'm going with you," he hissed as they headed down the hall toward the sitting room. "That dress is too... It isn't what an expert on modern manners should be wearing!"

Jessie stared blankly at him. What was his problem? she wondered in confusion as she glanced around at some of the women filling the huge drawing room they were entering. Her dress was about middle of the road, just as she'd planned. It was neither daring enough nor staid enough to cause comment. And Max had to be used to fashionable clothes. His last girlfriend had been a world-famous model. So why was he suddenly acting like a straitlaced puritan?

"Max, m'boy. Glad you could make it." A portly man hurried up to them.

"Good evening, Edwin. Jessie, this is Edwin Biddle, our host. Edwin, Jessie Martinelli, a business colleague. She's doing some consulting for my company." Max shaded the truth.

"Hello." Jessie smiled politely.

"Welcome to my home, Jessie," he said. "A beautiful woman is always a welcome addition to a party. And, Max,

I hope we can find a quiet moment to talk later. I have an investment opportunity I want to discuss with you. In the meantime, please help yourselves to a drink." He waved toward the bar set up in the corner of the room.

With an expansive smile Biddle moved on to the couple who had just come in behind them.

"Well, that answers the question of why he invited you," Jessie murmured. "Are you going to fulfill his expectations?"

"Only if it's to my advantage to do so. What do you want to drink?" Max took her arm and started toward the bar.

"White wine, please."

"Tell me," he asked in an undertone, "are there any unwritten rules about what I should be drinking at this kind of affair?"

"No, have anything you want, just don't have too much of it—but then, I don't have to tell you that."

"Why not?" he asked curiously. "You have no idea what my personal habits are."

"No, but I know what you've done with your life. And people who overindulge in alcohol do not build business empires."

"I see," Max said slowly, not sure how to take her words. He couldn't tell if she approved of his business accomplishments or not. But then, why should he care what Jessie thought? he asked himself. She was only a hired consultant. He wanted her expertise, not her good opinion.

The college-age bartender poured the drinks Max had asked for and handed them to him with a wide smile at Jessie, who was standing to Max's right.

Max gritted his teeth as Jessie smiled back at the man.

"You're supposed to be with me," Max muttered once they had moved away. "Don't flirt with the help."

"Don't be a snob," she shot back. "And I wasn't flirting."

"It certainly looked like it to me," Max grumbled.

"Either you need a new contact prescription or your education has been sadly neglected," Jessie said.

Max blinked as she suddenly stepped closer to him. An irrational longing to yank her into his arms and kiss her filled him, making him feel faintly desperate.

"If I were flirting…" She peeped up at him from beneath her ridiculously long brown lashes and gave him a sultry smile that would have ignited wet linoleum. "I'd do something unmistakably sexually provocative such as this."

Jessie reached out and ran the tip of her finger along his jaw, sending Max's heartbeat into overdrive. It was pounding so hard he was faintly surprised his shirt wasn't moving. As her finger touched his lips, he turned and captured it between them. He touched the tip of his tongue to her finger, and the taste of her filled his mouth, blurring his thoughts. He wanted to taste a whole lot more than just her finger. He wanted to ditch this party, take her back to his place and make love to her.

No. He hastily put a brake on his thoughts. He couldn't do that.

Jessie stepped back, hoping that he'd put her heightened color down to the heat in the room. It would be intolerable if he realized just how much his casual caress had affected her. She must have been out of her mind to have started something like that with a man as sophisticated as Max Sheridan.

"Hello, there, Mr. Sheridan." A husky voice snapped the tension that stretched between them. "I was so excited when Edwin mentioned that he'd invited you. I've been wanting to meet you ever since I saw you on a television show last year about the effect the European Union was having on our economy. I'm Honoria Farrington."

Jessie turned slowly and found herself looking at a tall,

gorgeous blonde wearing a friendly smile and a bright-blue dress cut just as low as hers.

"Are you interested in the Common Market, Ms. Farrington?" Max asked.

"Not at all," Honoria said cheerfully. "My interest was caught by the mention of your net worth. I decided then and there to hit you up for a donation to the North Shore Animal Shelter."

Jessie choked back a laugh at the woman's frank reply.

Max's expression was unreadable.

"I'm Jessie Martinelli," Jessie said. "Isn't that the shelter that doesn't kill the animals?"

"That's right," Honoria said. "Are you familiar with our work?"

"Not exactly, but I always mail them a donation when I watch the Westminster Dog Show in February."

"Good for you." Honoria smiled approvingly at Jessie. "Now, if we can just convince Max here to help…"

Jessie turned to Max to find him studying the woman with an intensity that sent a chill feathering down her spine when she remembered Max's penchant for blondes. Not only was this one gorgeous, but she had to be well connected or she wouldn't be here, and to top it all off, Honoria Farrington seemed to be nice.

"Honoria, Natalie asked me to tell you she needs to talk to you before you leave." A blond man in his midthirties joined them.

"Max Sheridan and Jessie Martinelli, this is my brother, Gerrick," Honoria said.

"Hello." Jessie nodded.

Max shook Gerrick's hand.

"Honoria, why don't you introduce Max to some of our friends while I make Jessie's acquaintance," Gerrick said.

Max's first impulse was to refuse to do anything that took him away from Jessie, but he reminded himself that he was here to meet eligible women, and Honoria Farrington certainly fit the bill.

Chapter Six

"Honoria, wake up!" Gerrick pulled open the faded drapes on his sister's bedroom window.

Honoria pried open one blue eye and peered shortsightedly at the delicate ormolu clock on her bedside table.

"Gerrick, it's seven o'clock in the morning, and I didn't get to bed until after two. Go away."

"Wake up, dammit. I've been doing some research this morning on Sheridan, and he's the answer to all our financial problems."

"He's going to invest in your biotech company?"

"I haven't approached him yet, but if we play our cards right, he will. While you were introducing Sheridan to our friends last night, I told his date, Jessie, all about the start-up biotech company. Hopefully she told him about it after the party. Sheridan didn't get to be a billionaire by being stupid. He'll recognize a great investment opportunity when he sees it."

"I hope so." Honoria suppressed a sigh. What was it about the men in her family? Every single one of them was obsessed, but at least Gerrick was obsessed with making his business a success, unlike her father, who'd been obsessed with gambling, or her grandfather and great-grandfather, whose drug of choice had been alcohol.

"Sheridan is the answer to everything." Gerrick began to pace across her bedroom floor. "If I can just get him to invest, the company will take off. Then you and Mother can have everything you ever wanted, and the Farrington name will be a financial force to be reckoned with in the city again."

"I already have everything I want," Honoria said, "and I don't think Mother ever will, no matter how much money she has at her disposal."

Gerrick sighed. "You could be right. Have you seen her latest credit card bill?"

Honoria echoed his sigh. "Gerrick, we've got to do something."

Gerrick rubbed the back of his neck. "What do you suggest? I tried canceling her cards, and she simply got new ones at a horrendous rate of interest. She's too old to change."

"She might not have much choice," Honoria said grimly. "This house is about her last asset. My entire paycheck wouldn't provide her with pocket money."

"That's why it's so important that you help me with Sheridan."

"Me? Why me? I don't know anything about what the firm does."

"Because I think I know why Sheridan was at the Biddles' last night."

"Because he was in the mood for a party?"

"Sheridan doesn't party. He always has an agenda."

"What could be his agenda?"

"Sheridan is a bachelor. A bachelor who came from poor white trash. And what is the first thing that poor white trash do when they finally make money? What was the first thing old Richard Farrington did back in the 1700s after he was given all that money for murdering the king's enemies?" Gerrick prompted at Honoria's blank look.

"Took off for the New World before the king decided he knew where too many of the bodies were buried and got rid of him?"

"And when he got here he took the quickest path to instant social acceptance by marrying into an old, established family," Gerrick said.

Honoria blinked. "Are you suggesting I marry Sheridan to get your funding?"

"Not if you don't want to, although I would think he'd appeal to any woman this side of senility. But all I'm asking you to do is to go out on a couple of dates with him. That will give you the opportunity to make a pitch to him to invest in the company."

"Gerrick, I'm not sure…"

"I wouldn't ask you to do it, but I've exhausted every other source, and we have to have a hefty infusion of cash or we're dead."

"Getting Sheridan to invest will not be easy." Honoria shivered at the memory of his remote blue eyes. He most definitely was not a man she would ever try to take for a ride. The landing would be guaranteed to be very bumpy.

"If you don't want to do it, I'll try to think of something else." Gerrick sounded defeated.

"I didn't say I wouldn't. I just think it needs to be handled very carefully. I was planning on hitting him up for a donation to the animal shelter, anyway. Maybe I could ask him out at the same time."

"Thanks, Honoria. You won't regret it, and in the meantime I'll see if I can learn anything from that Jessie he was with last night."

"Let me know if you discover anything useful," Honoria said. Gerrick was right. They had to do something. Either that or figure out a way to make her mother live within her means. Even she could see that tackling Sheridan would be a whole lot easier.

Jessie looked up from her computer as she heard the sound of her buzzer signaling that someone outside on the street was calling her. She glanced at the clock on her desk. It was too early for Max. He wasn't supposed to pick her up for another hour. Unless... Could he be so eager to see her that he was early? A flush scorched her face as she remembered the warm, slightly roughened texture of his jaw as she'd run her fingertips over it last night.

Or could it be that he had news he couldn't wait to give her? Like he'd found the woman he wanted to court? Jessie ignored the sinking feeling in the pit of her stomach the thought gave her.

The buzzer sounded again, and she jumped to her feet and hurried over to the intercom beside the door. There was no sense worrying about possibilities when she could easily find out for sure by answering it.

Depressing the talk button, she said, "Yes?"

"Jessie, open the door. I want to come up."

It was Max! She hastily hit the button to release the lock on the street door. Suddenly the day seemed brighter. Sharper. As if it had been repainted in more vivid hues.

Even if he'd brought news she didn't want to hear, at least he'd bought it in person.

The brisk rap on her door a few minutes later sent her heartbeat into overdrive, and she took several deep breaths on her way to open it, but the exercise did nothing to dampen her excitement.

With an escalating sense of anticipation, she swung her front door open, and her breath caught in her throat at the sight of him. The cream linen pants he was wearing seemed to emphasize the long, lean length of his legs, and the bright-blue cotton shirt lovingly molded his broad chest. If he ever lost his money, he could make plenty more as a male model, she thought. The man was sex on legs. Sex on long legs.

Before she could get a word out, Max said, "You didn't check to see who was there before you opened the door. Have you got a death wish? This is New York City."

Jessie gave him a thoughtful look and then slammed the door shut in his face.

"What the hell are you doing?" he yelled through the door.

"Practicing. You just told me not to open the door without being sure of who's there."

"The only thing I'm sure of is that you've lost your mind!" Max said. "Open this door."

"Who are you?" she called back, trying to keep the laughter out of her voice.

"I'm the man who's going to dock your paycheck if you don't open the door this instant."

Jessie swung the door open. "Economic reprisals do it every time. What brings you here this early?"

"Two things." He gestured with the white paper bakery bag and the yellow plastic sack he was carrying. "Make that three. Have you got any coffee to go with breakfast?"

"Sure, most of a pot, if you don't mind dark roasted."

"As long as it's not decaf," he said as he followed her out to her tiny kitchen. He sat down on a bar stool at her counter and watched as she poured him a cup.

"Black?" she said as she set it down in front of him.

"Uh-huh." He took a grateful sip and, opening the white bag, extracted a cheese Danish. "Have one," he said.

"Thanks." She reached into the bakery bag and pulled out an oversize apricot Danish.

"So tell me, to what do I owe the pleasure of your company, an hour early?" she asked.

Did she find pleasure in his company? Max wondered. He was certainly finding her company an unexpected source of enjoyment. He watched as she bit into the Danish, his gaze lingering on the tiny crumb of white icing on her upper lip. He found himself wanting to lick it away. And his compulsion unnerved him because he didn't understand it.

Jessie Martinelli was not the type of woman he was normally attracted to. For starters, her coloring was all wrong, and she was too short and her figure was not even vaguely lush. Not only that, but she was a great deal smarter than the women he normally dated. And a whole lot more focused. Hell, she even went to church and probably equated sex with love and marriage. Not his type at all.

But even though his mind could see all the inconsistencies, his body had been violently attracted to her since the first moment he'd laid eyes on her. His reaction to her was like a force of nature beyond rational thought. Even knowing that he absolutely couldn't get involved with Jessie didn't make the feeling go away.

Maybe he was going about this the wrong way, he considered. Maybe instead of fighting his compulsive attraction to her he should try giving in to it and see if that didn't dissipate the feeling. He wouldn't get in too deeply. Just share a kiss or two with her. A kiss didn't mean anything, he rationalized. It wouldn't raise expectations in her that he had no intention of fulfilling.

Yes, kissing her could be the answer to his problem. A sense of anticipation filled him.

"Leaverson called and left a message on my machine while we were at the Biddles' last night. He said a client had canceled his appointment this morning and if I wanted to he could meet us over at the house at eleven and take a preliminary look at it. I called him back first thing this morning and told him yes."

"Why do you need me there?" she asked, torn between the desire to be in his company and the sure knowledge that anything that bound her more closely to him was a mistake. She was already too aware of him as it was. She was beginning to understand what an artist friend had once told her about having difficulty selling her paintings because she had invested so much of her own emotions in them that it actually hurt to let them go. She was beginning to feel that way about Max. Even though she'd only spent a short time with him, he was demanding that she invest a great deal of effort into turning him into perfect husband material, and then she was supposed to turn him over to someone else. To someone who would probably see him as little more than a walking bank account. And Max deserved so much more than that in a wife.

"I told you before. I want a woman's input and at the moment you're the only woman on scene."

"Okay," Jessie said, unable to hold out against both her own urgings and his.

"Now then, about last night…" he began.

"What about last night?" she asked cautiously as she poured herself another cup of coffee. She definitely needed a second dose of caffeine to stay one step ahead of Max.

"I don't think that I made any social mistakes," he said slowly. "It was pretty much like every cocktail party I've ever been to. The only difference was the conversation was a lot more boring than usual. I got blow-by-blow accounts of a couple guys' golf games and a summary of some yachting race in Australia. And those were the highlights.

"What did you think of the party?" he asked curiously, wondering if that was the kind of social affair she enjoyed.

"Not much." Jessie saw no reason not to be frank.

"Why?"

Jessie frowned. "It's not that I'm not social exactly. It's just that I prefer to do my socializing with small groups of friends. Or, at least, among small groups of people with similar interests. With a crowd that large and noisy it was difficult to even carry on a conversation, to say nothing of finding a kindred spirit."

"I didn't much like it, either," he said absently, his mind trying to figure out exactly what she'd meant by a kindred spirit. A man? Had Jessie been trolling for a man last night? She'd damn well better not have been, he thought angrily. She could look for men on her own time, not his.

"You'd better learn to like, or at least tolerate, parties like last night's. If you marry a woman from Biddle's social world, it stands to reason that you're going to find yourself going to a lot of them."

Not a lot, Max thought, although some were inevitable. But how often would his wife want to attend parties? Once a month? Once every two weeks? Once a week? The thought of spending his weekends making inane conversation with some of the airheads he'd met last night was a distinctly daunting thought.

"On the other hand, you'll probably make a lot of good business contacts at those kinds of events," Jessie pointed out. She was certainly hoping to pick some up herself.

"Not really," he said. "The days when society was composed entirely of captains of industry are long gone. Besides, you can't talk about business in an environment like that party last night. Too much risk of being overheard."

Jessie blinked. "You mean industrial spying actually goes on at something like last night's affair?"

"I'm not sure I would call it spying exactly. More like picking up useful bits of information. A sharp businessman is always on the alert for information that can help him. Or damage his competition."

"There were a lot of loose lips by the time we left," she said. "One thing you can say about Biddle, he certainly wasn't stingy with his liquor."

"No, he wasn't," Max agreed.

Jessie took a deep breath and asked, "Did you meet any likely women last night?"

"No," he growled.

It was far too early in his campaign to narrow down the field, Max rationalized. It made more sense to keep all his options open until he felt comfortable with the social scene.

The surge of relief Jessie felt at his denial left her curiously weak for a moment.

"No one?" She persisted. "What about the gorgeous brunette who was coming on to you while that stockbroker was giving you the hard sell for some kind of artificial-cooking-oil options?"

"That was the stockbroker's wife," Max said dryly.

Jessie blinked. "Oh. What about the lady with the spec-

tacular violet eyes who kept asking you about San Francisco?"

"She giggled. Incessantly." Max shuddered at the
thought of hearing that annoying giggle at the breakfast
table for the next fifty years.

"I can see where that might get on your nerves," Jessie
sympathized, remembering a guy she'd once dated who'd
constantly sniffed.

"What about Honoria Farrington?" Jessie asked, trying
to sound casual. "On the surface, she's exactly what you
are looking for. Blond, good-looking and her family goes
back forever. Not only that, but she seemed like a really
nice person." Jessie forced herself to be honest.

Max frowned slightly as he remembered his conversation with Honoria. Jessie was right. Honoria had seemed
nice, but nice was such an anemic word. He might have to
settle for nice, but first he intended to try and find a woman
who was a little more… His eyes lingered on Jessie's
animated features. Sexier, he decided. He wanted there to
be a spark of sexual attraction between him and his wife
and there hadn't been with Honoria. She could have been
an eighty-year-old nun for all the sexual interest he'd felt
in her.

"It's early days yet," Max finally said as he reached for
a second Danish.

Did that mean that Honoria was an acceptable wife if
no one more appealing appeared? Jessie wondered. Or did
he mean that Honoria was unacceptable, and he was going
to continue his search? She didn't know, but instinct told
her to drop the subject. Harping on the subject of Honoria
would only serve to make Max more aware of her.

Jessie took another bite of her Danish.

When Max finished his sweet roll, he picked up the

yellow plastic bag and upended it on the counter. Several glossy magazines poured out.

Curious, Jessie picked one up. "Kitchens and bathrooms?"

"You said I should bring pictures of things that appealed to me and show them to the architect. So pick something out."

"But what does your apartment look like? I'm not the one who's going to be living in the house."

"Cream and brown. I told the decorator to make it restful, and that's what he came up with."

"Restful's good," Jessie said.

"Restful's boring. This time I think I'll opt for more color," he said.

"That certainly opens up all kinds of possibilities."

She climbed up onto the bar stool next to him and opened the first magazine to find herself staring at a kitchen that looked like it had been lifted straight out of a science-fiction novel.

"Impressive." Max nodded approvingly at all the stainless steel.

"Soulless." Jessie wrinkled her nose in disgust. "It looks more like a command center in a spaceship than somewhere to bake cookies."

"Do you bake cookies?" Max asked, diverted. He'd never actually seen a woman baking cookies. His mother had rarely been sober long enough to do anything more complicated than make coffee.

"Sure. I like baking," she said.

Max squinted thoughtfully as an image of Jessie standing over three small kids who were decorating Christmas cookies formed in his mind.

"Maybe I should make baking a requirement in my wife," he said.

"I suspect that would narrow the field rather drastically," she warned him. "Women today aren't heavily into baking."

"There's no reason they can't learn."

"There's no reason why we shouldn't have world peace, either, but I wouldn't hold my breath waiting for an excess of goodwill to break out! Besides, I suspect the problem is lack of time, not lack of inclination." Jessie tapped her finger on a picture. "Ah, now that is a kitchen."

Max looked down at the page, his attention riveted by the movement of her slender finger with its neatly trimmed nail that had been painted a soft pink. He swallowed uneasily as he remembered that finger moving over his jaw.

"What do you think?" Jessie asked.

Max forced himself to concentrate on the picture. It showed warm maple cabinets and a huge center island with a grayish marble top.

"That's a kitchen I can imagine a family working in," Jessie enthused. "Plus the warmth of the maple cabinets will help to offset the fact that you aren't going to have much natural sunlight in your kitchen."

"I'm not?" Max asked.

"No, because the only place to put in the kitchen is those three little rooms, and they all face north. So natural sunlight will be minimal."

"True," Max admitted. "Tear out the picture and we'll take it with us to show Leaverson."

"You don't want to look at any more kitchens?" Jessie asked.

"No," Max said. "All you need is one that works."

"I guess." Jessie carefully tore out the page and set it aside.

"Let's take a quick look at the baths before we leave," Max said.

Jessie obediently turned to the back half of the magazine and found herself staring at an old-fashioned claw-foot tub.

"Apparently reproductions are all the thing," she said after she read the caption beneath it.

"Not for me they aren't. I want the absolute latest in shower technology and an oversize tub with jets. One big enough for two."

Jessie swallowed uneasily as her mind obligingly supplied her with a picture of Max sitting in a tub of swirling water. Drops of water glittered on his skin and were caught in the crisp hair that decorated his chest. She took a deep breath, trying to control the almost overwhelming urge she had to reach out and touch him.

Surreptitiously she glanced over at him, her gaze lingering on his wide shoulders. It would almost be worth agreeing to a swimming lesson to see him stripped. She ran the tip of her tongue over her bottom lip as she imagined him in a pair of those tiny racing trunks.

"You don't agree?" Max asked, wondering at her odd expression. She looked...flustered, he finally decided, which was distinctly unlike her. Jessie was a very composed woman. Nothing seemed to ruffle her surface calm. In fact, she acted exactly the way he wanted his future wife to act. Like a lady, back when *lady* was defined as someone like Katharine Hepburn.

"Is that high-tech enough for you?" Jessie pointed to a picture of an oversize shower with water jets running up two sides of the stall. "I wonder how effective it is?"

"Very," he said. "I have one like that in my apartment."

Jessie stifled an envious sigh. "It sounds lovely. I make do with a single shower head. Maybe you should just tell Leaverson to use the latest gizmos in all the bathrooms."

"Okay," Max agreed.

"Well, that pretty much takes care of the kitchens and baths." Jessie reached past *Town & Country* and *Architectural Digest* to pick up the third magazine. *"Romantic Interiors?"* She read the title.

"I tried to get a cross section of decorating magazines," Max lied, having no intention of telling her that the minute he'd seen the cover picture of the elaborate four-poster bed with its fluffy cream satin comforter, he'd pictured Jessie sprawled across it. With that kind of mental stimulus he hadn't been able to resist buying the magazine, no matter how girly the title had sounded to him.

"Women are supposed to go for *Romantic Interiors* and since my wife will be spending more time at home than I will, I'm willing to put up with a bunch of frills," he said.

"Is a bunch of frills supposed to be compensation for confining her to the house?" Jessie said dryly.

"She's going to be the mother of my kids. Mothers stay at home with their kids."

"Thus spake Zarathustra! I've got a news flash for you, Max. Most mothers don't stay home full-time."

"They should," he said as an image of being met after school by a smiling woman wearing a loving smile and a plate of homemade cookies filled his mind.

"Why should a woman give up a career she's worked hard to develop to stay at home all the time?"

"Because she's their mother." Max repeated the words as if they were some kind of mantra. "Children need to have their mothers around."

"No, children need to have a caring adult around." Jessie wasn't even sure why she was arguing with him. If he wound up marrying some spoiled society woman she'd probably be only too glad not to have any outside demands on her time. But for some reason it was becoming personally important to her to make Max take an adult look at what she was beginning to think were ideas forged in his deprived childhood. He needed to see that having a mother like June Cleaver was not essential to raising happy, well-adjusted kids.

"My wife won't have a job outside the home," Max insisted. "That will be a precondition to our marriage."

"Simply because she doesn't have a job doesn't mean she'll be at home." Jessie tried another tack. "She'll probably belong to a dozen clubs and be active in several charities. I would imagine she'll be gone for large portions of every day."

Max felt a distinct chill at her words. He hadn't considered that angle. What else might he have missed in his eagerness to put his plan into effect?

"Don't look so fierce," Jessie said. "You simply need to reach an agreement about what the division of labor will be once you have kids."

"Is that what you intend to do before you get married?"

"No," Jessie said flatly, leaving him wondering if she meant no she wasn't going to negotiate or no she wasn't going to get married or no she wasn't going to have kids. He found the latter hard to believe. Jessie would be a natural with kids.

Before he could figure out a way to get her to elaborate on her statement, she changed the subject. "But to get back to decorating, I can't see you living with all this lace and satin."

Max eyed her curiously. "What do you see me living with?"

Jessie picked up a magazine featuring traditional interiors, flipped through it and pointed to a picture of a library decorated with leather furniture, an oriental carpet and sepia da Vinci ink sketches. "This reminds me of you.

Deep jewel tones, traditional, solid furniture and no annoying clutter of knickknacks."

Max looked down at the picture of the room she'd pointed to and nodded. "I like it. I can't stand fussy rooms, and I hate having to move a bunch of things off an end table in order to put a cup of coffee on it."

"You could decorate everything but the master bedroom and leave that for your bride to furnish as she likes," Jessie said slowly.

"Where am I supposed to sleep in the meantime?" Max demanded.

"That house is going to have lots of bedrooms. Pick one of the others."

"No." Max pulled the *Romantic Interiors* toward him. "I want the bedroom to look like this."

"The point isn't what you want," Jessie said patiently. "It's what your bride wants."

"Don't you like it?"

Jessie took a closer look at the room pictured. Actually, she really liked it. It appealed to something deep inside her. She could almost feel herself snuggling up under that silky comforter with Max. She shivered as goose bumps popped out on her arms. She also had no trouble imagining a couple of little kids jumping into the bed on Saturday mornings.

"It would probably appeal to most women's feminine fantasies," she finally said. "But you aren't marrying most women. You are marrying one particular woman, and she might not like it."

"If she doesn't like it, then I'll just find someone else to marry," Max said, feeling inordinately cheerful for some reason.

Jessie shook her head. "Why do I have the feeling you're on a collision course with disaster?"

"You're a natural pessimist?"

She could well be, Jessie thought glumly. As Maggie, her childhood friend, had once said, her childhood would have forced Pollyanna to rethink her outlook on life.

Max's cell phone suddenly beeped, and he got to his feet. "Time to go. Fred will be meeting us downstairs in five minutes. You bring the pictures."

"Yes, sir," she muttered at his preemptive tone. She kept forgetting that Max was a very high-powered businessman, and then he'd suddenly start issuing orders and forcibly remind her.

Jessie gathered up the magazines and followed him out, pausing only to grab a sweater and her purse.

"It's July," he said. "You don't need a sweater."

"I wasn't thinking of the outside temperature," she said as she locked the door. "For some reason people tend to keep the inside temperature as cold as charity."

And it didn't come much colder than that, Max thought grimly. But it was odd that Jessie had used that expression. He studied her serene features as she entered the elevator in front of him. From the look of her, she couldn't know much about being on the receiving end of charity. She undoubtedly came from a solid middle-class family who had never known real economic problems. Her father was probably a professional and ten to one her mother was a housewife.

Once they had reached the street, she glanced around, looking for Fred and the Mercedes. Ice suddenly chilled her skin as she caught sight of an older woman with graying red hair at the corner who was studying her apartment house. At the sight of Jessie the woman took a step toward her and then paused as if uncertain.

Jessie hurriedly averted her gaze, not wanting to attract the woman's attention. It couldn't be her mother, she assured herself. The woman had only a superficial resemblance to what her mother had looked like the last time Jessie had seen her, fifteen years ago. But even if the woman's face looked vaguely familiar, her clothes sure didn't. Her mother had always gone in for flamboyant skintight clothes that had had one objective: to attract masculine attention. The woman walking toward them was wearing a pair of white slacks and a pale-blue silk camp shirt. Her mother wouldn't have been caught dead in such a sedate outfit.

"Here's Fred," Max said as the Mercedes pulled up.

Jessie hurriedly scrambled into the car. She wanted to get out of here. She didn't want to know if it was her mother. And she most definitely didn't want Max to know. Her mother would never be able to resist making a big play for a man as gorgeous as Max.

If Max ever found out just what her background really was… A shiver of fear slashed through her, shortening her breathing and making her feel faintly queasy. He'd be bound to think that someone with a past like hers couldn't possibly be a suitable mentor. He'd get rid of her so fast her head would spin. Everything she had been able to find out about him had pointed to a man who was absolutely ruthless in the pursuit of a goal. And that was just a business goal. How much more ruthless would he be in chasing his long-cherished vision of the perfect family?

Chapter Seven

"I think you'll be very happy with your home once we've finished." The tubby little architect beamed happily at Max as he bounced down the front steps.

"I don't know about that, but I guarantee you that he'll be happy considering what he intends to charge you," Jessie murmured to Max as she watched Leaverson wedge his portly frame into the small BMW he had parked on the street in front of Max's town house.

"It isn't that much," Max said.

"Compared to what? The national debt? I still think that you ought to get a second opinion. And maybe a third and a fourth one, too."

"You said he was the best," Max told her.

"Yes, but…"

"I can afford the best," Max said with bone-deep satisfaction. "I have no intention of cutting corners. This is where I intend to raise my family. I want them to remember having lived in a house that was perfect in every way."

Turning, Max pulled the front door closed behind them and then locked it. "Let's go find a restaurant and have lunch," he said.

Jessie fell into step beside him. "I think you're wrong."

"No, I'm not. I'm starved."

"Not about needing food. About memories. Kids don't care about houses. I didn't."

What she did remember was the hundreds of broken promises her mother had made. She remembered the humiliation of always having to make excuses for her mother's nonappearances at school functions. And the embarrassment she'd felt when the neighbors would stop talking when they saw her. A thousand hurts were indelibly carved in her memory, but the public housing she'd spent her childhood in she could barely remember.

"That's probably because you didn't grow up in a two-room shack. Hell, we didn't even have indoor plumbing, and to reach the door you had to pick your way through the junked cars in the front yard. I used to lie about where I lived so no one would know." Max's features hardened at the memory. "My kids are going to have a home they can bring their friends to without feeling ashamed."

She glanced up at him and winced at the anguished memories she could see reflected in his eyes. Despite the undeniable success he'd made of his life, his childhood still haunted him.

"You need to let the past go," Jessie said impulsively. "Your parents were obviously two people who were overwhelmed by life, but that was their problem, not yours."

"Don't be ridiculous. I don't care about the past."

"If you don't care, then why are you trying so hard to live your life exactly the opposite of the way they did?" Jessie persisted.

"I'm not." His arctic tone froze off the discussion, and Jessie wisely let it drop. He was paying for social expertise, not for psychological insights into his character.

"Is this place okay?" Max stopped in front of a small restaurant tucked in between two much larger buildings.

"Looks fine to me." She followed him inside and slipped into one of the empty booths.

They had just finished ordering when Jessie's cell phone rang. Pulling it out of her purse, she checked the number. She didn't recognize it.

"Aren't you going to answer it?" Max asked.

Deciding she might as well, she said, "Hello."

"Jessie, this is Gerrick. Gerrick Farrington. We met last night at the Biddles' party, remember?"

Jessie considered telling him that she remembered him only too well. That giving her a twenty-minute lecture on the wonders of biotech made him very memorable. Although probably not in the way he preferred.

"I really enjoyed talking to you last night," Gerrick continued, and Jessie had the odd feeling he was reading from a script. But why? She was as positive as she could be that she hadn't raised a spark of passion in him. In fact, she'd give good odds that all his passion was reserved for his company.

"I'd like to take you to that new nightclub everyone is talking about. That is, if you're free tonight?" His voice was clearly audible to Max.

Jessie watched as Max's jaw tightened in annoyance and he shook his head at her. "You're working tonight," he told her.

Far more curious about what Max had planned than she was in anything Gerrick had to say, Jessie moved to end the conversation. "Sorry, Gerrick, I have a previous engagement, but thanks for the invitation."

"But I'm sure you'll enjoy the club."

"I'm sorry," Jessie repeated, refusing to be drawn into justifying her decision. "Now, if you'll excuse me, I have to go."

"But—" His voice was sliced off when Jessie cut the connection.

"Boyfriend?" Max demanded.

"No," Jessie said slowly. "Gerrick Farrington, from the Biddles' party last night."

"I take it he didn't make an impression on you?" Max probed.

"Oh, he made an impression, all right," she said dryly. "I never date men whose idea of a good time is to carry on monologues about their work."

"Then why do you look so…" Max struggled to quantify her expression.

"I don't know what I look like, but what I feel like is confused," Jessie said. "First, I'm curious about where he got my cell number. Second, that phone call doesn't mesh with his behavior last night."

"Why do you find it so hard to believe that he could have taken one look at you and fallen madly in love?" Max asked, curious at the way her mind worked.

Jessie gave him a long, thoughtful look that forcibly reminded him of a fifth-grade teacher he'd once had who'd immediately seen through every excuse he'd ever tried on her. "First of all, it isn't love you fall into at first sight, it's lust. Second, I am not the type of woman to inspire sudden, overwhelming emotion in a man." She sighed. "I think maybe it's all the curls. I tend to remind men of their little sisters or their third cousin once removed."

He didn't know about other men, but he didn't have any little sisters or any cousins no matter how removed they were. As far as he was concerned, those curls were sexy as hell! Not that he had any intention of telling her. Theirs was a business relationship.

"I thought all women believed in love at first sight." Max grabbed the chance to find out more about her.

"Not once they get past sixteen. Tell me, what do you have planned tonight that would have interfered with my accepting Gerrick's invitation?" Jessie determinedly changed the subject. Talking to Max about love was making her very uncomfortable.

"Did you want to go out with him?"

"Nope, just curious."

Max felt something relax inside him at her words. He didn't want her dating until he'd gotten himself safely engaged. Men would only distract her, and he was paying for her exclusive attention.

"I have tickets to a charity dinner tonight. The place should be crawling with acceptable women."

"What's the dinner in aid of?" Jessie asked as the waitress brought their orders.

"I have no idea. My P.A. bought the tickets. We're not going for fun. This is work."

"Right, work." Jessie leaned back slightly as the waitress set her tuna-fish sandwich in front of her.

"Do you have something to wear tonight?" Max hungrily took a bite of his hamburger.

"I'll wear the dress I had on last night," Jessie said. "For what you paid for it, I'd have to wear it to every social event for the next ten years to get your money's worth out of it."

"You can't wear it again. A lot of the same people who were at Biddle's party should be at the dinner."

"So?" Jessie asked. "I'm not trying to impress them. You are."

Max blinked at the acerbic tinge to her voice. "I am not trying to impress anyone."

"That's not what it looks like from where I'm standing."

"This isn't about me. This is about my kids. I have a plan."

"Yeah, well, you know what they say about the best-laid plans."

"Not my plans. My plans come to fruition," he insisted. "And as for your plan of wearing the same outfit, forget it. We'll go and buy something else this afternoon. In fact, we'll buy a couple of somethings so you'll be prepared."

"Okay." Jessie gave in. Clothes had been part of the deal.

As soon as Jessie had finished her coffee, Max hit the pager for Fred.

Once they were in the car, Max gave Fred an address a few blocks from Bloomingdale's.

"Where are we going?" Jessie asked.

"To a dress shop I know of," he said and then pulled out his cell phone and spent the traffic-clogged ride accessing his messages.

Jessie spent the time speculating on how he knew about the dress shop. She didn't like any of the answers her imagination suggested.

Twenty minutes later Jessie found herself in a small boutique. The floor was covered with an inch-thick silver carpet and against the walls were racks of colorful outfits.

"May I help you, Mr. Sheridan?" The stick-thin saleslady gave Max a warm smile.

"Spend a lot of money here, do you?" Jessie muttered to Max.

He gave her a repressive look, and turned to the saleswoman. "Yes, we would like to see a selection of evening gowns. In something other than black. Jewel tones, I think."

"Of course, Mr. Sheridan."

The saleswoman hurried over to a rack and began to sift through it.

"Why no black?" Jessie asked. "This is New York. Every woman I know wears black. Some of them exclusively."

"So you'll be different."

Jessie grimaced and yanked on one of her curls. "I already am different, thank you. I prefer to blend in. As much as possible," she added as he raised his dark eyebrows in disbelief.

"You aren't a sparrow. You're a bird of paradise. Live with it," he said.

Jessie blinked, trying to decide if that was a compliment or not. Probably not, she finally decided. One didn't have to think about compliments. One knew instinctively what they were.

"Here we are." The saleswoman rushed back with four gowns draped over her arm. "I think these will do very nicely. Why don't you come with me, madam, and try them on."

"I want to see them before any final decisions are made," Max ordered.

"Yes, sir." Jessie slipped into her "please the client at any cost" mode.

"Mr. Sheridan is right," the saleswoman said once Jessie had slipped on the first dress. "You do look spectacular in jewel tones."

"I look nice," Jessie corrected her. "I wouldn't look spectacular if I were draped in diamonds."

The saleswoman looked thoughtful and then said, "Certainly not spectacular in the same way as his last girlfriend. He brought her in here all the time. Now, she was a beautiful woman by anyone's standards, but there was a hard edge to her that…that repelled," the woman finally said.

"In order to be truly memorable a woman has to have more than just looks. There has to be something inside that shines through. Class, if you will, and it has nothing to do with your net worth or your ancestors.

"Mr. Sheridan has it," the woman continued. "He always talks *to* me and not *at* me, if you see what I mean."

"Yes," Jessie agreed, knowing exactly what the woman meant. Max saw people. Saw them as distinct individuals and treated them as such.

"Go show him that dress," the woman urged her.

Taking a deep breath, Jessie went out of the dressing room.

Max's whole body clenched as he caught sight of Jessie. Desire ripped through him, threatening to tear his composure to shreds.

As soon as he could find an appropriate moment, he'd kiss her, he promised himself. And once he'd actually kissed her, he'd undoubtedly discover that it was the same as kissing any other woman, and he'd be able to concentrate on what was really important. Finding a wife.

"What do you think?" Jessie asked as she looked down at the deeply cut neckline. It was certainly fashionable. She just hoped that wherever they were holding the fund-raiser didn't keep the air-conditioning turned up high or she'd freeze.

Max eyed the dress critically. Any man seeing that outfit was going to want her, and men coming on to her would distract her from what she'd been hired to do. No, that dress was out.

"For the price of these dresses you'd think the designer would be willing to use enough material to cover all the relevant parts," he grumbled.

Jessie frowned slightly. Where was Max coming from? This gown was on the conservative side when viewed next to what his last girlfriend had normally appeared in public wearing. So why the disapproving frown on his face? Unless...

Could it be because he thought of her as the hired help, and the help didn't wear clothes in the forefront of fashion? Jessie studied his disgruntled expression. But if that were true, then why bring her here in the first place? There wasn't an unfashionable garment in the whole place. It didn't make any sense.

"I like that emerald-green color on Jessie," Max told the hovering saleslady. "Just not the dress. Try for something a little more…" He gestured with his hand, and Jessie's eyes followed the forceful movement of his large hand. "There."

Jessie didn't argue with him. The dress was in essence a uniform that he was paying for. Within reason, he could have what he wanted. Although… A brilliant splash of scarlet hanging on the rack caught her eye on her way back to the dressing room, and she paused to hastily check the size. Gleefully she grabbed it.

"I must say," the clerk said, "that Mr. Sheridan does not seem to be his normal self today."

"Oh?" Jessie said encouragingly.

"He never objected to what any of the other women he brought here chose." The woman eyed Jessie with more interest. "In fact, he sounds more like a possessive husband than a boyfriend."

A flash of longing engulfed Jessie at the woman's words. A longing she immediately repudiated. She absolutely couldn't begin to daydream about Max. Not only was he totally unavailable, but he wanted kids. And she could never risk passing on her tainted genes to some unsuspecting infant. And as for the mistakes she'd be bound to make raising a child… She barely suppressed a shudder.

"How about trying this one next?" The saleslady called Jessie back from her thoughts.

"I want to try this one on." Jessie hung the bright-red

dress she was clutching on a hook in the dressing room and began to slip out of the rejected emerald dress.

The clerk looked at the dress, glanced up at Jessie's bright red curls and barely suppressed a shudder.

"It is a gorgeous gown. Ralph Lauren," the clerk said slowly. "And the long slender cut would show off your figure to perfection. However…"

"And while the top leaves one shoulder completely bare, it does entirely cover up my breasts." Jessie ignored the woman's less than enthusiastic expression.

"It should be restrained enough for Mr. Sheridan, but it's so…"

"So?" Jessie's voice was muffled as she slipped it over her head. The sensuous silk material slid down over her body like a benediction, hugging her curves without being blatant about it.

When the clerk made no effort to help her, Jessie zipped it up and then studied herself in the mirror.

"No doubt about it, Ralph Lauren is a genius. It looks even better on than it does off, and that's saying something," Jessie said with satisfaction.

"But it's so…so red," the clerk burst out. "And with your hair…"

"I've always wanted to wear red," Jessie said, trying to ignore the way the scarlet clashed with her hair, "but I never had the nerve."

"Listen to your nerves," the clerk urged her. "They're telling you something important."

"Let's see what Max says." Jessie pushed aside the curtain and stepped outside the dressing room.

"What do you think?" Jessie opened her arms and twirled around.

Max chuckled. "That you can moonlight as a traffic light."

Jessie grimaced. "That bad, huh?"

"The dress is a perfect fit." Max's eyes followed the supple line of the dress down her body. "And I certainly like the style. Does it come in any other colors?"

"No, but I do remember an aqua one from Lauren that came in this morning," the clerk said. "Let me see if it has been unpacked yet." She hurried toward the stockroom.

Jessie sighed. "Back to the drawing board."

"Hurry up and try on the others. We're running behind schedule."

"It's Saturday. You don't have schedules on Saturday."

"I have schedules every day of the week."

"Your wife might have something to say about that," Jessie said as she went back into the dressing room. One thing was clear, his wife had better have a strong personality or she was going to find herself totally swamped by Max. He'd apparently never heard of a compromise. She could foresee some stormy times ahead in his marriage. Unless his wife didn't care enough about Max to even argue with him.

For some reason the thought made her feel sad. Max had so much to offer a woman, and yet all he was actually prepared to give was his money and his services as a lover in order to ensure children. It was a recipe for disaster, as far as she could see. But she also couldn't see what she could do about it. He was paying her for technical advice, not marriage counseling. Which was a good thing, because she wasn't qualified to give it. She'd never even *seen* a successful marriage close up.

Jessie twisted around as she struggled to pull down the dress's zipper. It refused to budge.

Of course it was jammed, she thought in exasperation. Max was in a hurry. Otherwise there would have been no problem.

Opening the dressing-room door, she cautiously stuck out her head.

"What's the matter?" Max demanded.

"Have you seen the saleslady?"

"No, she's probably still in the stockroom. Why?"

"My zipper's jammed, and the material's far too fragile to try forcing it."

"Turn around," Max ordered.

Jessie's first craven impulse was to retreat back into the dressing room and wait for the saleslady, but her pride wouldn't let her. She absolutely refused to act like some repressed spinster from a bygone age when she knew herself to be a modern, sophisticated woman.

Taking a deep, sustaining breath, Jessie slowly turned around, presenting her back to Max.

He moved closer, and her heart lurched and then began to race madly as the heat from his large body crowded her. It seeped through the thin silk of her dress, making her skin feel too tight for her body.

Jessie caught her lower lip between her teeth and tried to force her intense physical awareness of Max back into her subconscious, where it couldn't hurt her. She lost the battle the moment she felt the pressure of his fingers against her shoulder blades.

"There's a thread caught in it," Max said. "I'll have it free in a minute."

His fingertips brushed against her neck, and she shivered as an intense longing to press herself against him gripped her. She froze, trying to contain the tremors racing through her. She couldn't bear for him to realize just how strongly she was reacting to his casual touch.

"There," Max muttered as he finally freed the zipper. A second later she felt cool air flowing across the heated skin of her bare back. It was immediately followed by the feel of Max's warm hands as they slipped beneath the edges of the dress to cup her shoulders.

"You have the softest skin," he murmured against her hair. "Like satin."

Jessie struggled to drag air into her lungs past her constricted throat. Her eyes instinctively slid shut to better savor the sensations flowing through her.

Disoriented, she stumbled slightly as his hands tightened and he turned her around to face him.

Jessie risked a look up and was immediately lost in the swirling depths of his eyes. They seemed to glow with some emotion that her mind was too confused to decipher. Thinking had suddenly become an impossible challenge. All she could cope with was what she was feeling.

She watched with an escalating hunger that threatened to consume her as his mouth came closer. Instinctively, her entire body strained upward, desperate to make physical contact with him.

As his mouth brushed lightly against hers, she felt the remaining threads of her self-control snap, freeing her to move deeper into his embrace. Hunger tore through her. A hunger that owed nothing to logic or common sense. A hunger that was primal, drawn from the very core of who and what she was.

His arms suddenly tightened around her, and he yanked her up against his hard body as his mouth crushed hers.

Jessie's throbbing body jerked in reaction as she felt the tip of his tongue tracing over her bottom lip. Eagerly she opened her mouth to give him access—an access he was quick to take advantage of. His tongue surged inside to explore the heated depths.

A frustrated, yearning sound escaped her as she was

consumed by a powerful awareness of her own body. An awareness that acted like a drug, blinding her to the fact that they were standing outside the dressing room of a store. Her only concern was the necessity of feeding the intoxicating sensations.

With a suddenness that made her feel bereft, Max released her and stepped back. Confused and shaking with reaction at the sudden cessation of the intense pleasure she'd been feeling, Jessie ran the tip of her tongue over her swollen lips. Her confusion grew as she watched Max follow her tongue's movement with an intensity that shook her. If he was still unsatisfied, then why…?

"I think you'll really like this dress." The saleslady's voice broke into Jessie's muddled thoughts, bringing reality crashing in on her.

What was she doing? Jessie wondered in horror. She knew that getting involved with Max would be the height of insanity. So why had she practically thrown herself into his arms? The only answer that occurred to her—that she couldn't help herself—did nothing for her battered self-esteem.

Grateful, she allowed herself to be shepherded into the dressing room.

With fingers made clumsy by her slowly fading passion, she took off the gown and hung it back on the hanger, being very careful not to catch the saleswoman's eye. Jessie didn't know if the woman had seen that explosive kiss, nor did she want to know. All she wanted to do was to buy the dresses and escape from the scene of what had to rank as one of the most stupid acts of her life. To pretend it had never happened.

Maybe she could, Jessie considered. Max would certainly cooperate. Because from his perspective, nothing much had happened. A snatched kiss in a shop wouldn't mean a thing to a man like Max. For that matter, it shouldn't have meant all that much to her, either. So why had it? She didn't know. Nor was she sure she wanted to know. She had a nasty suspicion the answer would prove to be devastating to her long-term peace of mind.

Chapter Eight

Max froze as he watched Jessie emerge from her apartment house and walk across the sidewalk toward him. The beading on the aqua dress she was wearing caught the waning sunlight, splintering it into minuscule prisms that sent sparks of color dancing over her pale, perfect skin. His breathing fractured, and heat began to pour through him as he watched the sensual sway of her body beneath the thin silk.

"You look…" Fantastically hot, he thought. Sexy enough to raise his blood pressure fifty points.

He could almost feel the texture of her soft mouth beneath his as his mind insisted on replaying the kiss they'd shared earlier. It was as if all the kisses he'd ever had up to that point had merely been preparation for that kiss with Jessie.

But how had she felt? The uneasy thought intruded. Had she found it as mind-blowing as he had? He didn't know. He knew she'd responded to him. What he didn't know was what her response meant.

So where did he go from here? he wondered. He didn't have an answer. Hell, he wasn't even sure what the question was. Maybe his best bet would be to back off and let things cool down between them.

"One generally chooses an adjective that is complimentary," Jessie said when he made no effort to finish his sentence. Oddly enough, the fact that Max was ill at ease helped to calm her own agitated nerves. Maybe he wasn't any more comfortable with the memory of that shattering kiss than she was.

"I think I prefer competent." She tried to sound impersonally professional.

A smile curved Max's lips at her prim expression. "How about wholesome?" he said.

"Yuck!" Jessie wrinkled her nose in disgust. "That makes me sound like a glass of milk."

Max chuckled. "If you wanted extravagant compliments you should have worn an extravagant gown."

"How could I? You refused to buy the emerald gown. Now that was…"

"Indecent." Max scowled at the memory of the dress's daring décolletage.

"Nonsense, it was just a little provocative. I always wanted to be a little provocative," she said wistfully. "But when you have freckles, people typecast you as the girl next door."

"Trust me, that emerald gown went beyond provocative. Hell, a woman might as well go naked as wear that."

"Naked isn't all that sexy," Jessie said.

"Where'd you get an idiotic idea like that?" Max glanced up the empty street.

Jessie followed his gaze, frowning slightly when she realized the car wasn't there. "Where's Fred?"

"Going around the block. There was a patrol car standing in front of the building next to yours when we arrived. Double-parking didn't seem like the brightest idea."

"True. It's also true that totally naked isn't that sexy. My friend Maggie and I went to Europe last summer, and one of the places we visited was a nude beach in Spain."

"You went nude on a beach!" Max glared at her, inexplicably annoyed at the thought of her exposing herself for all and sundry to gawk over.

"Nah, I haven't got the confidence to do it. But the point I'm trying to make here is that it wasn't sexy. When we first got there, I was embarrassed and then curious and finally bored."

Max stepped toward the car as Fred pulled up and yanked open the back door of the Mercedes.

"Stay off nude beaches!" he ordered.

Jessie slipped into the backseat, wondering what it was about her that seemed to bring out Max's prudish streak. Her curls? Her freckles? Or could it be a remnant from his childhood in the deep South?

"Hi, Fred." Jessie greeted the driver.

"Evening, Ms. Martinelli," Fred responded, never taking his eyes off the street outside.

Jessie could feel the heat from Max's large body crowding her as he followed her into the car. It seeped into her muscles, making them feel pliant. As if he could mold her into anything he wanted. But he couldn't change the past. He couldn't miraculously give her the background she needed to be an effective mother. He couldn't change her genetic propensity for addictive behavior. The unpalatable truth depressed her.

"Don't look so sad," Max said. "If you really want to take up nude swimming, I'll take you to my place in California outside San Francisco."

"Anyone who goes nude in San Francisco runs the risk of frostbite. And besides, I don't swim. I simply sit in the sun."

"And court skin cancer?"

"Hey, what can I say? I like to live dangerously. I've even been known to eat whipped cream on my hot fudge sundaes."

Fred snorted, and Max glared at the back of his head.

"But enough of my walk on the wild side. Brief me about this evening." Jessie purposefully tried to move the conversation onto what he had hired her to do. Maybe if she were to concentrate on business, she would be able to think of him as a client instead of a devastatingly attractive man whose bones she wanted to jump.

"According to my P.A., it's a fund-raiser for the arts," Max said. "Most of the city's social and business elite will be there."

"Excellent. There should be lots of eligible women for you to look over." Jessie forced herself to sound cheerful.

"Yes," Max clipped out.

Jessie shot him a surreptitious glance out of the corner of her eye, trying to figure out what kind of mood he was in. She wasn't sure. Maybe he was simply nervous about the coming event. After all, if things went well he might meet his future wife tonight. That would be enough to unnerve any man. She ignored the sensation of loss that swept through her. She didn't care, she assured herself. Max was just one more client in a long line of clients.

Thirty minutes later Fred pulled up in front of the opulent hotel where the fund-raiser was being held.

"Don't move until I check it out," Fred said.

Jessie watched as he got out of the car and carefully

scanned the crowd. "What on earth does he expect to happen in front of a hotel?" she asked.

"I don't know. I pay him for his expertise, so I try not to second-guess him, even when I find his extreme caution irksome."

Fred opened the door beside Jessie, and she hastily climbed out before he changed his mind. Max was apparently of the same mind for he quickly joined her on the sidewalk.

"I'll page you when I want to be picked up," Max told him.

Fred scowled at the milling people. "I could stay with you," he suggested.

"No." Max vetoed the idea. "We'll be okay. There's going to be a former president, a couple of senators and all kinds of diplomats from the UN. Security will be really tight."

Fred grimaced, his expression saying more clearly than words that he didn't trust anyone's security but his own.

"See you later, Fred." Jessie gave him a sympathetic smile. Being professionally paranoid in a crowd like this must be the pits.

Jessie instinctively inched closer to Max as someone bumped into her from the back.

"Let's get inside." Max put an arm around her and forced his way through the mass of people in the lobby toward the ballroom.

"I hate crowds." Max sidestepped an elderly lady who sailed past them.

"Being seen at these kinds of affairs are bread and butter to a lot of the society crowd," Jessie pointed out. "I would imagine you'll go to at least a couple a month after you're married."

"They don't want me," Max said cynically. "They just want my checkbook. I'll have to put a stipulation that I won't go to something like this more than twice a year into the contract."

"What contract?" Jessie asked.

"The prenup. I told you—I've got more brains than to marry a woman without proper safeguards."

Jessie opened her mouth and then closed it when she found she had nothing to say. She could hardly give him a lecture on true love since he wasn't marrying for love, true or otherwise. Nor was she qualified to give the lecture. There'd been precious little love of any kind in her life to date.

"You sure can put the damper on the happily-ever-after scenario," she finally said.

"There is no happily ever after. Just like there are no fairy tales."

"Depends on the fairy tale. I'm certainly not waiting for a mythical Prince Charming to ride off into the sunset with me."

"Why not?" Max asked, curious at the way her mind worked.

"Any man who would marry a woman simply because she had the right shoe size is a brick short of a full load. Who knows what else he might do."

Max grinned. "I never thought of it quite like that. And apparently neither have generations of romantic women."

"First of all, not all women are romantic. I'm certainly not. Second, even if I were, romance is a lousy basis for marriage."

"We're in agreement on that."

Jessie bit back the urge to tell him that as far as she was concerned, marrying to create the perfect stereotypical family was even dumber than marrying someone because their foot fit the shoe. He was the client, she reminded herself. Clients were allowed to be as stupid as they wanted to be as long as they paid her fees on time.

But in Max's case it was a waste of a totally gorgeous hunk of masculinity, she thought as they finally made it into the ballroom.

Max glanced around the room, which was filled with large round tables, each set for twelve people.

"Do we have assigned seating?" Jessie noticed that most of the tables were already full.

"No, all we need to do is find…"

"Jessie, Max!" Gerrick's voice sounded aggressively cheerful to Jessie.

She plastered a social smile on her face, mentally bracing herself for yet another monologue on the joys of biotech.

"Good evening, Gerrick," Jessie said.

"You should have said you couldn't go clubbing with me this evening because of work." Gerrick gave her a warm smile that sat oddly on his tense face. "Personally, I hate these kinds of affairs." He glanced around with a frown. "I usually just mail them a check, which is all they want anyway. I'm only here because Honoria's date came down with the flu at the last minute.

"Honoria, look who I found." Gerrick partially turned, and Jessie realized that his sister was behind him.

"Hi, Jessie, Max." Honoria gave them a warm smile that made Jessie feel like a really nasty person. Honoria was just plain nice, and yet Jessie still didn't want to be anywhere near her.

Jessie stole a quick glance at Max to find him studying Honoria with a thoughtful expression that filled her with a growing sense of dread. Could he be considering Honoria for his wife? Just because he hadn't mentioned it to her didn't mean he wasn't.

"You must sit with us," Gerrick aimed the words somewhere between Max and Jessie. "I can finish telling you about my biotech firm."

Now there was an incentive, Jessie thought. Was that why Gerrick had asked her out? Could his start-up need an infusion of cash, and he was hoping that she might have some influence with Max?

It was possible. From the little she knew about start-ups, they always seemed to be short of cash. But it really didn't matter what Gerrick's motives were, she told herself. What mattered was that she ensure that Max had the opportunity to spend the evening with Honoria. That was what she was being paid for.

"Thank you, we'd love to sit with you and Honoria," she said.

Max shot her a sharp glance, wondering why she'd accepted. Was she not as indifferent to Gerrick as she'd claimed?

Jessie trailed along behind Gerrick toward a table on the far side of the room, wishing the evening were ending and not just starting. She wasn't sure which scenario promised to be worse. Watching Max pursue Honoria or being bored to death by Gerrick.

Honoria was worse—she answered her own question. Gerrick was just an annoyance, while Honoria… The thought of Max and Honoria together sent a shaft of pain lancing through her.

She was going to have to turn Max over to another woman soon or later, she reminded herself, and that explosive kiss had shown her that sooner would be much better. She needed to bow out of his life before she did something monumentally stupid like fall in love with him.

Once they were seated, Honoria introduced them to the other people already at the table.

"This is Bitsy and Ed Worth and Amber and Jared Smythe and Natalie Browne and Wilson Delacroix. This is Max Sheridan and Jessie Martinelli."

"Martinelli is an Italian name." Bitsy looked intrigued. "So where'd the gorgeous red hair come from?"

"Out of the family gene pool. My ancestors come from Venice, and we tend to blondes with green eyes or redheads with brown."

"That's right," Amber said. "According to legend, the Phoenicians were supposed to have settled Venice, weren't they?"

"Actually, there is solid historical evidence to support the theory," Jared said. "I saw a special on PBS a while back, and Italy is surprisingly diverse. We here in America tend to think all Italians are dark with olive complexions because most of our immigrants came from southern Italy."

"Yes, professor." Honoria grinned at him, and Jessie began to relax. Maybe the evening wouldn't be such a trial after all.

"Honoria, it's your turn to get the drinks," Gerrick said. "Why don't you take Max with you to help carry?"

Was that Gerrick's game plan? Jessie wondered, remembering how he'd all but shoved Honoria into Max's arms the night of the Biddles' party. Was Gerrick trying to market his sister to Max? She had absolutely no idea.

"What would you like to drink, Jessie?" Max's voice pulled her out of her tangled thoughts.

"White wine, please," she said.

"I'll be right back. Don't move," Max ordered before he left.

Jessie set her evening bag down on the empty chair to her left to save it for Max.

Gerrick slipped into the empty seat on her right and opened his mouth, but before he could say anything, Bitsy spoke up.

"What do you do, Jessie?"

"Besides date the most gorgeous male I've seen in years," Natalie purred.

"Thanks," her escort snapped.

"Hey, I tell it like it is," Natalie shot back.

"Max and I aren't dating. I'm a business consultant, and I'm setting up a series of workshops on business etiquette for his midlevel and upper management." Jessie took advantage of the opening to plug her business.

Amber blinked. "You mean like Miss Manners?"

"I wish," Jessie said dryly. "I don't publish anything. Mostly I deal with businesses. So much business is international these days, and manners can be a real pitfall. You can mortally offend someone from another culture and never even realize it."

"It sounds fascinating," Jared said.

"It has its moments," Jessie agreed.

"So why are you with Max?" Gerrick slipped the question in. "From what I've seen, his manners are fine. I wouldn't think that he would need any private tutoring."

"I'm gathering data on the kinds of affairs that his top executives would normally attend so that I can plan my workshops." Jessie gave him the cover story she and Max had agreed upon.

"Jessie, I'm sending a delegation in September to China to drum up business for my company," Ed said. "Could you do a workshop on Chinese manners as they relate to business? With the market as tight as it is, I need every advantage I can get."

"Certainly." Jessie felt a glow of satisfaction. At least

this part of her plan was working out. She was picking up useful business contacts.

"Here." Ed handed her his business card. "Call my office next week, and we'll set up something."

"I'm going to mention your workshops to my kids' school principal," Amber said. "At the last parent-teacher meeting we were discussing the appalling manners of some of the kids."

"I do work with a couple of private schools in the area," Jessie said.

Gerrick's cell phone suddenly rang and he hurriedly got to his feet. "Excuse me. I need to take this."

"No doubt business." Amber shook her head at Gerrick's retreating back. "That company of his is consuming him."

Ed frowned. "I get the nasty feeling that it's consuming a whole lot more than just his time."

"Did he ask you to invest more, too?" Jared asked.

"Yes, but the two hundred thousand I've already given him is the limit I can afford. And I have the worrisome feeling that it's going to wind up as a tax write-off."

"Shh!" Bitsy hissed. "Honoria's coming."

Jessie looked up just as Max set a glass of white wine down in front of her.

"Thank you." Jessie watched as Honoria slipped into her seat. Try as she might, Jessie wasn't able to read anything on Honoria's impassive face. Had Max made a move on her while they'd been alone? Or had Honoria been the one to make the move? Or was all the maneuvering on Gerrick's part? But what good would it do for Gerrick to scheme to bring his sister and Max together if Honoria wasn't willing? And, if he did want them together, what was his ultimate goal?

Jessie resisted the impulse to rub her forehead, which was beginning to ache.

The lights dimmed as Max sat down beside her.

Jessie turned toward the stage as the master of ceremonies took the microphone and gave them a pep talk about the good that the arts did.

After a pudgy man in a dog collar had given a brief blessing, the waiters started serving dinner.

"I approve of a charity that doesn't waste its money feeding its donors," Max whispered in her ear.

Jessie choked on the tough piece of chicken she had been attempting to swallow. She grabbed her water glass and took a quick gulp and then frowned at Max over the rim.

"Don't say things like that," she muttered. "Especially don't say things like that when I'm eating."

"Why not? It's the truth."

"Let me be the first to disabuse you of the rather quaint notion you seem to be harboring that the truth has a high priority in social interactions," Jessie said.

"Translate that," he said.

"Lie your head off and you'll get along just fine with your fellow man."

Max eyed her for a long moment and then said, "But what about my fellow woman?"

Jessie stared into his eyes, mesmerized by the tiny lights she could see dancing deep in them. A shiver danced over her skin, raising goose bumps. What did he mean by that? Or did he mean anything? Maybe he was simply making conversation. Jessie ran the tip of her tongue over her suddenly dry lips, and her stomach twisted as his eyes followed her tongue's movement with utter absorption. Suddenly the memory of their kiss seemed to quiver in the air between them.

"Have you marked the item you're going to bid on, Max?" Amber's voice snapped the tension vibrating between them.

With a monumental effort, Jessie turned her head, breaking eye contact with Max. It took an almost physical act of will to accomplish it. She stared blankly at her plate for a long moment, oddly grateful for the interruption. For a moment there, she had forgotten everything but how Max made her feel, and that was dangerous. Both to the job she was supposed to be doing and to her own peace of mind.

Jessie picked up her copy of the catalogue by her plate and made a show of looking though it while she struggled to region her composure.

"I don't want anything," Max began, and Jessie hastily shoved her leg against his. Heat poured through her at the enticing contact. He felt hard and muscular, the way men were supposed to feel and so seldom did.

Max, never slow on the uptake, hastily rephrased, "But I will buy something, of course, since it's such a worthwhile cause."

Jessie smiled approvingly at him. One of the things she liked about Max was that he was a quick study. A very quick study.

"Tell me." Max grinned ruefully at Jessie. "What is it I'm going to buy?"

Before Jessie could respond, Natalie suddenly spoke. "What about the necklace on page six?" She held up the catalogue to a full-page picture of a chunky diamond and emerald necklace.

"Isn't it spectacular?" Natalie cooed with a sidelong look at Honoria's still face.

Jessie felt a prickle of unease. She could almost feel the tension tightening around the table. She glanced at Natalie's avid expression, recognizing the source of the tension but not the reason for it. She wasn't left in ignorance for long.

"Old Von Storch's widow donated it for the tax write-off," Natalie said. "It's an English antique that one of the early dukes of Devonshire gave to one of his mistresses. Honoria can tell you more, can't you, dear?"

When Honoria simply gave Natalie a vague smile, Natalie continued, "It's an old family heirloom of the Farringtons, Max. Honoria's grandfather about five times removed gave it to his wife when their son was born. Her father lost it in a poker game, of all things. The first of his many, many losses."

Natalie gave Honoria a pseudosympathetic smile.

The sudden silence at the table was deafening, and Jessie wanted nothing so much as to fling the contents of her wineglass in Natalie's smug face. But giving in to the impulse would only make an embarrassing situation worse.

"Personally, I like the quilt on page three." Jessie deliberately changed the subject. "I intend to bid on it."

"I'll buy it for you." Max supported her effort.

"No, thanks," Jessie said.

"Whyever not?" Natalie said.

"I make it a policy never to accept gifts from clients. I've found it saves misunderstandings in the long run," Jessie said.

"Oh, there's no possibility of a misunderstanding," Ed said with an annoyed glance at Natalie. "Everyone knows what the situation is."

No, everyone did not know, Jessie thought in annoyance. She felt as if everyone had been given a script to read except her, and she hated the feeling. It brought back memories of junior high school, when she was always on the outside, looking in.

To Jessie's relief, the auctioneer pounded his gavel for silence, and she turned toward the stage as the man started auctioning off the first item. The bidding was brisk as a lot of the lesser items went quickly. When the auctioneer held up the colorful quilt Jessie had admired, she put in a bid for it and was successful.

She turned to Max with a triumphant smile.

"Congratulations." Max smiled back at her.

"What are you going to do with that thing?" Natalie said. "No interior designer would touch it."

"I like it," Jessie insisted. "It's cheerful."

"It certainly is that." Amber chuckled. "In a color-blind sort of way."

"Be quiet," Natalie hissed. "He's about to auction off the necklace."

After announcing a reserve bid of one hundred thousand dollars, the auctioneer opened the bidding. It was brisk, quickly rising to half a million. It hung there for a few seconds when Max suddenly threw in a bid of six hundred thousand.

Jessie was caught by surprise at his unexpected action. Why was he bidding on the necklace? She glanced at his impassive face. There was no answer to be read there. Jessie stole a quick look at Honoria, who looked impossibly remote. Could Max be buying it for Honoria? Jessie wondered with a sinking feeling in the pit of her stomach. If he'd made up his mind to marry her, returning the family jewels as a wedding present would be a nice touch. Romantic, even. Jessie tried to ignore the hurt she felt because she was far too interested in Max herself.

Chapter Nine

"Jessie?"

Jessie heard the strained voice the moment she emerged from her apartment building the following Monday.

Automatically she turned toward the voice and found herself face-to-face with her mother for the first time in fifteen years. A dizzying kaleidoscope of violent emotions cascaded through her, sending her stomach into free fall as she struggled to reconcile her last image of her drunken, screaming mother with this neatly dressed middle-aged woman standing in front of her.

"Jessie, I know you're upset with me," Cecilia Martinelli began.

A gust of anger shook Jessie at her mother's choice of words. Upset? Upset didn't come within light years of describing the pain and anguish of her mother's betrayal.

"You have to listen to me," Cecilia pleaded. "I've changed. I want a relationship with you."

"It's too late. I just want to be left alone," Jessie insisted. "The time is long past for us to forge any kind of relationship."

Jessie slipped around her mother, hailed a cruising cab and stumbled into it, collapsing onto the backseat.

She gave the driver Max's business address and then closed her eyes, trying to shut out the image of her mother's face. Been there and done that, Jessie told herself as old memories bubbled to the surface of her turbulent thoughts. Memories of her mother sobbing about how sorry she was that she'd spent the grocery money on alcohol or occasionally some man she'd picked up in the street. How many times during her childhood had Jessie heard the familiar litany of "I'm so sorry. It won't ever happen again. I promise you, Jessie. I swear on your grandmother's grave." And every single promise her mother had ever made had been broken.

And now her mother was trying to start the game all over again. But this time Jessie didn't have to play, she told herself. This time she wasn't a defenseless child. This time she had choices, and her first choice was to never allow her mother to hurt her again.

"Here you are, miss." The driver double-parked in front of Max's office building.

Jessie hurriedly paid him and scrambled out, pausing a minute on the sidewalk outside the impressive double doors to try to bring her skittering emotions under control. She took a deep breath and then a second when her heart continued to pound. This was business, she told herself. She had to project a calm, competent front.

But how much longer would she be working for Max, Jessie wondered as she entered the opulent lobby.

Had the fact that he'd bought the Farrington necklace

on Saturday night been a signal that Max was going to marry Honoria? Was Honoria the reason Max had called early yesterday morning and canceled their plans for the day? Was that why he'd told her to meet him in his office this morning?

Jessie bit her lip to hold back the sudden pain that pierced her at the thought.

She should be glad if Max had picked such a nice person to marry, Jessie tried to tell herself. Her brother might be a bore, but that was hardly Honoria's fault. As Jessie knew only too well, you couldn't pick your relatives.

So why wasn't she pleased? Jessie probed her reaction as she crossed the bustling lobby toward the elevators. Why did the thought of Max with Honoria make her feel faintly desperate?

It wasn't a question she was sure she wanted answered.

"Hi, Max." Honoria tried to keep her nervousness out of her voice as she entered Max's office. She could do this, she encouraged herself. All she had to do was to lay the groundwork for Gerrick to make his own pitch to Max. Gerrick deserved to make a success of his company, and if someone didn't invest a large sum of money and do it fast, the company would collapse, taking Gerrick's hopes and every cent they had remaining with it.

"Good morning, Honoria," Max said, studying her as she walked toward him.

On the surface Honoria was exactly what he was looking for in a wife. So why did she leave him cold? He didn't have a clue. All he knew for certain was that she could have been someone's sixty-year-old aunt for all the sexual response she raised in him.

He struggled to imagine Honoria holding a child, but the

image wouldn't form. Instead a picture of Jessie cradling a grubby little toddler with ink-black hair popped into his mind. The baby had chocolate smeared across its chubby cheeks and a huge grin on its face. The grin was matched by Jessie who was beaming down at the child as if it were the most precious thing in the world. Maybe to Jessie her children would be, he thought. The middle class was noted for raising their own children. They didn't hire nannies to do it for them. Not only that, but Jessie would be able to give her husband lots of pointers on raising kids. Jessie was a fantastic teacher.

"To what do I owe the pleasure?" Max asked Honoria.

"I was in the neighborhood and decided to stop by and take you out to lunch so that I could hit you up for a donation to the North Shore Animal Shelter." The words she'd practiced in front of her mirror that morning. They sounded as lame in his office as they had in her bedroom. With an effort, she kept the smile on her face.

Max smiled politely and pulled his checkbook out of his gray suit jacket, which was slung over the back of his chair. "I'd be more than happy to make a donation to any charity that Jessie supports. Unfortunately I'll have to take a rain check on lunch."

Max wrote out a check and handed it to her.

Honoria accepted it and shoved it, sight unseen, into her purse. "On behalf of a lot of fuzzy little animals, thanks, Max."

"Let me walk you to the elevator." Max started toward the door, and Honoria allowed herself to be politely ushered out. According to Gerrick, timing was everything, and this clearly wasn't the time to try to interest him in the company.

Jessie looked up as the elevator doors began to open on the fifty-second floor and flinched when she saw Honoria emerge from Max's office. Hastily Jessie punched the button to reclose the doors, and then randomly hit a button for a lower-level floor. She didn't want to meet them until she'd had a chance to erect some defenses. It was one thing to suspect that Max had settled on Honoria as his wife and quite another to come face-to-face with the fact.

What exactly had they been doing in his office? she wondered. Had Max been kissing Honoria the same way he'd kissed her?

A searing pain shafted through her, making her shiver.

The very intensity of the pain acted as a curb on her chaotic thoughts, helping her to regain control. She had no right to object to anything Max did, she told herself. Certainly the kiss they'd shared didn't give her the right.

It didn't matter that somehow she'd started thinking of Max in nonprofessional terms. What mattered was that Max hadn't done the same. To Max she was simply the consultant he had hired to polish him up to find a wife. And even if by some miracle he did see her as a desirable woman, nothing could ever come of it because she didn't even come close to fulfilling his requirements in a wife. She winced as she remembered her earlier meeting with her mother. Actually, he would be hard-pressed to find someone who was further from his ideal. If only… Jessie hastily cut off the thought.

Jessie got off the elevator when it stopped on the third floor and slowly walked the length of the hallway, determined to give Honoria time to leave before she returned.

Ten minutes later she felt in control once more. Calm and cool and ready to face any number of shattering announcements by Max. Getting back into the elevator, she again punched the button for the fifty-second floor. This time when the doors opened, there was no one in sight.

Jessie closed her eyes, took a deep breath and slowly walked toward his office.

"You're late." Max's deep voice flowed across her already agitated nerve endings, making her feel edgy.

Jessie glanced down at her watch. "Only five minutes." She waited for him to tell her about Honoria, but to her confusion he didn't say anything. Did that mean that he hadn't chosen Honoria? Or did it mean that he wasn't ready to tell her yet, for reasons of his own? It was also possible that Honoria's being in his office this morning had nothing to do with Max's plans and everything to do with Gerrick's. Her spirits lifted slightly at the thought.

Max gestured toward the chair in front of his desk and said, "Have a seat. I just need to double-check the wording in the contingency clause of this contract, and then we'll go to lunch. I want to go over Saturday night. It would have been better if we could have done it yesterday, while everything was still clear in our minds, but by the time Parnell and I finished working on the Chinese deal it was after midnight."

"I can wait in the outer office," Jessie offered, feeling almost boneless with relief at the news that Max hadn't canceled their plans to spend yesterday with Honoria.

"I won't be long. Sit down."

Feeling a bit like the family dog, Jessie sat down on a chair and pulled out of her purse the paperback she was currently reading.

"You keep a book in your purse?" Max said in surprise.

Jessie blinked. "Certainly. I spend a lot of time waiting for buses and clients."

"When did you start carrying a book?"

Jessie shrugged. "I have no idea. I've always had my nose stuck in a book."

"Did your mother teach you that?" he asked, realizing

how few hard facts he had about her background. Getting personal information out of Jessie was harder than getting a politician to take a firm stand.

Jessie suppressed a wince. The answer was yes, but not for the reason Max meant. Jessie had used books as an escape from the sordid reality of her world. And as she'd gotten older, the habit of reading had become as ingrained as brushing her teeth.

"Yes," she finally said. "Children should be encouraged to read. Television should be kept to an absolute minimum."

Max's eyebrows rose. "You don't like television?"

"No," Jessie said bluntly. "Do you?"

"I don't know. I've never had time to watch anything other than the news and business reports."

"I would imagine you get your full quota of pathos and bloodshed in the business world. You hardly need more marketed under the guise of entertainment."

Her breath caught in her lungs as Max grinned at her, his eyes sparkling with humor. "There is that, but at least the bloodshed in the business world is metaphorical. Now quit trying to distract me or we'll never get to lunch."

"Me!" Jessie squeaked in outrage. "I was…" She hastily clamped her lips together and opened her book.

Two minutes later she gave up trying to make sense of the printed page and surreptitiously glanced over the top of her book at Max.

His head was bent as he studied the paper in front of him. The light pouring in through the window behind him gave his hair an almost bluish sheen. His broad shoulders were encased in a crisp white cotton shirt, and his blue-and-gray striped tie had been yanked down to allow him to unbutton the top button on his shirt. His shirtsleeves had been rolled back to expose his muscular forearms.

Jessie ran the tip of her tongue over her suddenly dry lips as she focused on the black hair on his arms. Her fingertips trembled with a sudden compulsion to yank his shirt out of his perfectly tailored gray suit pants and run her hands up under it. To explore the exact texture of his muscular chest. She wanted to touch him so badly it was like a fire raging in the mind. Burning away social convention and inhibitions alike. She craved physical contact with him because… Because she was head-over-heels in love with him, she realized in horror.

She wasn't! Jessie instinctively tried to deny her appalling insight. She absolutely, categorically refused to be in love with Max Sheridan. She couldn't love him. She hadn't known him long enough. Love took time to grow. To develop. She stared down at the deep-blue carpet at her feet and tried to steady her pounding heart. She refused to be in love with Max Sheridan. Being in love with him was a one-way ticket to disaster, because there was no way he was ever going to fall in love with her. To him she was his image consultant. Period.

Even the fact that he'd kissed her didn't mean anything. To a sophisticated man like Max, a kiss was nothing.

"Is something the matter?" Max's deep voice interrupted her muddled thoughts.

"No!" Jessie bit out. "No," she repeated more calmly, struggling to sound like her normal self. She absolutely couldn't let him discover how she felt. Her self-esteem would never survive the humiliating blow of him pitying her.

"By the way, I was finally able to set up an appointment for your sailing lesson," she said hurriedly, changing the subject. "It's tentatively scheduled for next Saturday, and my knee should be healed enough for another tennis lesson in a couple days."

"How about a swimming lesson?" Max asked.

"Maybe by next week." Jessie put off the evil moment. "Are you finished with…whatever it is you're doing?"

"For the moment. I need to get Finance to double-check some of these figures. They look pretty blue sky to me."

"There's something to be said for optimism," Jessie offered.

"What?" Max asked as he rolled down his shirtsleeves and rebuttoned his cuffs.

Regretfully, Jessie watched as his muscular forearms disappeared from view.

"What do you mean, 'what?'" she asked.

Max paused in the act of putting on his suit jacket, and Jessie stared at the way his shirt stretched across his broad chest. If she were to just slip free a couple of those buttons, she could slip her hand inside his shirt and… Her mouth began to water.

"You said there was something to be said for an optimistic viewpoint, and I asked what it was. Are you sure you're all right? You sound spaced to me."

"I told you. I'm fine." Jessie dragged her gaze away from the temptation of his chest and focused on his face. "And I think optimistic people are a lot more fun to be around than pessimistic ones."

"Depends." Max straightened his tie. "In business any company not prepared for a worst-case scenario going in won't be coming out."

"I suppose," Jessie conceded.

"Do you have a disaster plan for your business?" Max asked.

"I'm going to take that bonus you promised me and use it as a financial cushion," Jessie said as she followed him out the door.

"Fifty thousand?" Max scoffed. "That's not a cushion. It's barely even a ground sheet. You must have other plans?"

Her only plan after Max was going to be how to recover from a devastating case of unrequited love, she thought grimly. She had the horrible feeling that once Max was out of her life, he was going to take with him any chance she might have had for long-term happiness. She was never going to find a man who could even vaguely approach Max for looks or personality or drive or sexiness. After having known Max, any other man would be a very distant second choice. What was it they said? Life was a bitch and then you died. For the first time Jessie was in total agreement with the sentiment.

"You need a backup plan for your company." Max followed her into the elevator and punched the button for the ground floor.

"What makes you think I want to spend my entire life teaching manners?" she said, annoyed that he seemed to see her as some kind of dedicated career woman with no outside interests. "I may get married and cut back to part-time."

Max was taken completely by surprise by the violent surge of emotion that ripped through him at the thought of Jessie married. Of Jessie belonging to some man. Of Jessie being pregnant with some man's kid. Some other man's kid. Of *course* she'd eventually marry. He tried to tamp down his raging anger. Jessie was a fascinating, sexy woman who would bring a lot to any relationship. The wonder was that she was still single.

Jessie's private life wasn't his concern, he told himself. He had a plan. A plan he'd been working toward his entire adult life, and he wasn't going to be deflected from it now, no matter how sexually alluring Jessie was.

"About that dinner Saturday night," he began.

"We can talk once we get to the restaurant," Jessie said, hoping that she would be in a more settled frame of mind by then.

The restaurant Max took her to was an upscale place with leather banquettes and subdued lighting. It made Jessie think of snatched meetings between lovers.

"Casablanca," she muttered as she followed the middle-aged hostess to their seats.

"What about it?" Max asked once they were seated.

"This place," Jessie said. "For some reason it makes me think of Humphrey Bogart."

Max allowed his eyes to roam over the tables filled with men in hand-tailored suits. "Somehow I can't see Bogie here. On the other hand, Ingrid Bergman would have fit right in."

"Ingrid Bergman would have looked at home in the middle of a civil war. She had enough class to transcend her surroundings."

"Why?" Max asked curiously.

Jessie shrugged. "Maybe training, but I suspect she was simply born with presence. Some people are. You were."

Max shot her a startled glance. "Thanks. I think."

"No reason to thank me. One collects certain gifts at birth, courtesy of your ancestors. It isn't anything to be proud of. Or ashamed of, for that matter. It simply is. What's important is what one does with those gifts."

"An interesting philosophy," Max said slowly, having never considered the situation from that angle before.

"Would you care for a drink?" The waiter appeared at their table.

"Nonalcoholic strawberry daiquiri," Jessie said.

"Coffee, black," Max said.

"I don't think heredity is as simple as you make it out to be." He returned to their conversation.

"On the contrary. I've found that life can usually be boiled down to the basics. It's only when people try to rationalize their actions that things get complicated."

"I don't have to rationalize my actions," Max said, sensing criticism.

"Certainly not to me. Although you might find yourself trying to explain to your kids somewhere down the road why you don't love their mother."

"I will respect their mother," Max insisted.

"And what will happen if she decides she wants love?" Jessie persisted, knowing she was risking really teeing him off, but unable to stop. Somehow she had to make him examine what he was doing. Really examine where his chosen course of action might lead him in a few years.

"How do you think we're going to have kids?"

With a monumental effort, Jessie managed to blank out the devastating thought of Max in bed with another woman.

"That's sex. Anyone over the age of puberty knows the two don't necessarily go together. Or are you trying to tell me you've been in love with every woman you've ever had sex with?"

"You don't think I might fall in love with my wife after I marry her?"

Jessie gritted her teeth against the agony that shot through her at the idea of Max in love with someone else. Someone who couldn't possibly appreciate him half as much as she did.

"Possibly. Did you meet anyone at that charity dinner who appealed to you as a wife?" she forced herself to ask, even though she shrank from having her suspicions confirmed that he was seriously considering Honoria as a wife.

Max thought a moment. The only face he could recall with any degree of clarity from the party was Jessie's. The other women there had faded into insignificance beside her. Maybe it was the brilliance of her hair that made her memorable. Or maybe it was because she didn't bore him with inane chatter. Or maybe it was her sharp mind and insightful comments. Whatever it was, Jessie had easily wiped the images of the other women from his memory. Even Honoria, whom he'd seen just a few minutes ago, was only a fuzzy memory.

"What about Clarice?" Jessie asked.

He frowned. "Who was Clarice?"

"She was the brunette whom you met at the door as we were leaving."

"I don't remember her," Max said truthfully.

"Okay, how about Emma? She was the one who came over to speak to Bitsy after the auction."

"She was dressed like an octogenarian. She was so buttoned up she's probably sexually repressed.

"Unlike Gerrick," Max added, grabbing the opportunity to probe her reaction to the man. "The guy was coming on to you all evening long."

"Not exactly," Jessie said slowly.

"What do you mean?" Max asked.

Jessie shrugged. "I think Gerrick has his own agenda, and it doesn't have anything to do with me personally."

"Maybe. So how do you rate my performance at the dinner?"

"Your table and social manners were perfect, and your clothing was superb. I think the only thing that still needs work is your fund of small talk."

"It's bankrupt," he said dryly.

Jessie grinned at his rueful expression. "Not entirely. You just don't seem to have mastered the knack of talking to people who aren't overly bright."

"That reminds me. About your protégé," Max said.

Jessie braced herself for bad news about Luis.

"We actually found him a slot where I think he can be productive."

Jessie blinked in surprise, trying to figure out where a disadvantaged teenager who couldn't read could fit into Max's organization, let alone be productive. She couldn't.

"Luis had been helping maintenance out and was over in marketing. He saw part of a presentation on Walter's desk."

"Who's Walter?" Jessie asked.

"The head of marketing. The presentation was for a new MP3 player that's being marketed to preteens. Luis made a couple of good suggestions about appealing to the Hispanic portion of the target audience. Walter promptly stole him off maintenance as an advertising trainee."

Jessie nodded thoughtfully. "It makes sense. If anyone should be able to tell you how to appeal to a Hispanic teen, it would be a Hispanic teen. How does Luis feel about it?"

"The job came with a raise. He likes it just fine. Plus that part of marketing tends to be a little unconventional. He'll fit in better down there than he would in some other areas."

"Good." Jessie felt a sense of relief, now that Luis and his family appeared to be safe for the foreseeable future.

"I've been thinking," Max said slowly.

"About what?"

"I originally interviewed three of your protégés."

Jessie held her breath, mentally willing him to offer them a job, too. A company as big as Max's could absorb dozens of teenagers like Luis and never even notice. But the suggestion had to come from Max. Max wasn't the sort to be coerced into anything.

"According to Walter, Luis is going to be an asset, and

he was by far the least promising of the lot. Maybe I could give the others jobs."

"That's a great idea," Jessie enthused. "The other two are still in school, but they could work full-time now and on vacations and part-time when classes are in session."

Max frowned as he stared off into the middle distance. "We've never hired part-timers before. Maybe we ought to set up an internship program. A small internship program," he amended when an ecstatic squeak escaped Jessie.

"Small," she hastily agreed. "And when they're through school, you can hire them full-time."

"If they work out and if we have openings," Max corrected. "I'll call Human Resources and have them get in touch with you."

"Me?"

"They're your lame ducks. Besides, you're the teacher. You'd be able to give Human Resources ideas on how to handle it. Just include the hours you spend on my bill."

"No." Jessie shook her head. "My work with the kids at the center is part of my ticket of admission."

Max frowned. "Ticket to what?"

"To the human race. I believe that you have to give something back. You can't just take. My work at the center is the way I give back."

An interesting concept, Max thought. And very like Jessie, he realized. Jessie was one of life's givers, not one of the takers.

Chapter Ten

"This is a hell of a way to waste a Friday afternoon," Max grumbled as he glanced around the bustling hotel lobby.

He shifted restlessly, and the fragile teacup he was clutching in his large hand rattled.

"Be careful," Jessie warned. "Causing a scene is bad manners in spades, and I assure you that dumping your tea on this place's overpriced carpeting would make every last waiter in the vicinity come running."

Max scowled. "I'd like to get my hands on the sadist who came up with the idea of afternoon tea. And what the hell is in these things?"

He picked up a tiny sandwich from the plate on the coffee table in front of him and glared at it.

"Cucumber and watercress," Jessie said. "Traditional afternoon tea staples."

"They wouldn't fill up an anorexic. It's a good thing I'm not hungry. I'm going to refuse to attend teas. I'll put it in the prenup."

"At the rate that thing is growing, you're going to have to print it in volumes like the encyclopedia," Jessie said. "But I wouldn't worry overmuch. It's unlikely that anyone is going to ask you to attend afternoon tea. At least not until your kids are in school."

"What does education have to do with this kind of social torture?"

"A lot of the private schools have regular afternoon teas for parents."

"My kids aren't going to a school that has teas. If they're willing to torment the parents like that, I don't even want to think what they might be doing to a bunch of defenseless kids behind my back."

"You haven't had much to do with modern kids, if you think they're defenseless. Besides, a lot of parents really like teas. It gives them a chance to talk to the other parents and teachers in a relaxed setting. Rather like an afternoon version of a cocktail party."

"I don't like cocktail parties, either. Give me one good reason why any rational human being would waste an afternoon juggling a cup of tepid tea and disgusting sandwiches."

Jessie shrugged. "Maybe to emulate the English upper classes? Maybe because they can afford to take the time off work? Who knows."

"Who cares?"

"You do. You need to master the little things so you can move on to the big things. The list of which is headed by finding a wife."

Max grimaced. It was proving harder and harder to remember his original goal. In fact, when he was around Jessie he found it impossible to concentrate on anything but her.

"I'm beginning to wonder if this was such a great idea," he said, giving voice to his growing doubts.

"Nonsense. Anyone who can juggle as many financial irons as you can surely manage to handle one cup of tea and some small talk."

Max didn't correct her assumption that he was talking about this ridiculous tea party she brought him to.

"I hate small talk." He seized on another grievance in a day that seemed chock-full of them. "I can't seem to get the knack."

"I've noticed. But I have hopes that you'll improve. If for no other reason than that it is a good business asset."

"Actually, selling a superior product at a competitive price is the biggest asset."

Jessie chuckled. "I take it modesty is not a prerequisite in big business?"

"People tend to take you at your own evaluation."

Jessie eyed him thoughtfully for a long moment and then said, "If you truly believe that, then why are you trying to create a different persona for marriage?"

"That's not it exactly."

"Then what is it exactly?" Jessie asked, willing him to open up.

Max stared down into his teacup for a long moment. He preferred not to tell her that he wanted a society wife so he could flaunt her like some kind of hard-won trophy. Putting his motivation into words somehow made it seem tawdry. Instead he gave her part of the truth. "My mother was an alcoholic who dabbled in drugs when she could afford them. She was also into sexual excesses, and she wasn't the least bit discreet about it. I spent my childhood being whispered about as the son of 'that woman.' I swore that when I had kids no one would ever have cause to whisper about them behind their backs. That they'd have a mother they could be proud of."

Jessie winced at the lingering pain she could hear in his voice. Max's childhood sounded every bit as harrowing as her own had been. Maybe even more so. At least she had finally escaped into the relative stability of a foster home after her mother had gone to jail. He hadn't even had that comfort, meager as it was.

But even understanding where Max was coming from, she still felt he was on a collision course with disaster, given his ill-conceived plan for finding a wife. Somehow, she had to shake him out of his preoccupation with the past and make him view the whole situation through the eyes of the adult he now was.

"You'd have done better to have vowed to give your kids parents who loved each other," Jessie persisted.

"I doubt very much if kids know if their parents love each other," Max said. "Or particularly care as long as both parents are around. Kids are remarkably self-centered."

Jessie stilled as the memory of her mother's anguished features flashed through her mind. Was she being self-centered by refusing to have anything to do with her mother? For a moment a shiver of doubt shook her, but she shook it off. It wasn't the same thing at all. No sane person would ever contemplate getting emotionally involved again with someone who had caused them so much pain.

"I'll grant you that kids tend to be self-centered, but they are also very alert to atmosphere and tension, and I would think that it would be a bit tense living with someone without love." Jessie focused on Max's problems and not her own.

"Careful, you're beginning to sound like a romantic," Max said.

"And you sound like you watched one too many *Leave*

It To Beaver reruns when you were a kid," she said tartly. "Let me be the first to break it to you, Max. June Cleaver was one writer's idealized vision of what a housewife should be. Nobody, and I do mean nobody, cooks dinner in heels, pearls and a twinset these days."

"I am perfectly aware that June Cleaver is fiction. But I see no reason why my kids can't have a mother who will meet them after school with cookies. It doesn't matter who baked the cookies. What matters is that their mother is there to listen to them. To sympathize about their problems and celebrate their victories.

"I certainly can't do it. I'd probably do permanent psychological damage to them if I tried parenting on my own. I need someone with experience of a normal childhood to be my interface with my kids."

"But what do you consider normal?" she asked. "Most of the people Biddle socializes with were probably raised by nannies. Is that what you want to pass on to your kids?"

"No, but—"

"Goodness, I do hope we're not interrupting anything." Natalie's voice came from behind Jessie's chair. "You sound almost…strident, Jessie."

Jessie bit back an urge to say something satisfyingly vulgar and turned to find Natalie accompanied by an embarrassed-looking Honoria. She shouldn't really be surprised to see them, Jessie thought in resignation. The reason she'd brought Max here was because it was a favorite afternoon haunt of the social elite.

Jessie's eyes narrowed as she watched Natalie smile seductively up at Max, who had politely risen to his feet. He really did have excellent manners, Jessie thought with a sense of pride. The kind of manners that took into consideration other people's feelings. The fact that he had trouble juggling a teacup and a cucumber sandwich at the same time was irrelevant.

Jessie bit down hard on the inside of her lip as Natalie suddenly reached out and ran her hand down the length of Max's striped silk tie. It was all Jessie could do to stop herself from grabbing Natalie's useless-looking white hand with its luridly painted red claws and flinging it away from him. She wanted to tell Natalie in no uncertain terms that Max belonged to her and to keep her greedy hands off him.

But how did Max feel? Jessie wondered as she watched his face for a clue as to what he was thinking. She couldn't read anything in his expression. It was an urbane mask that could be hiding anything from intense pleasure to extreme anger. He could even be thinking that Natalie was the embodiment of his dreams of the perfect wife. But if that were the case, then why wasn't he encouraging Natalie? Was he hoping that her interest would be piqued by his reserve? Or was it that his interest lay in Honoria and for some reason he wasn't ready to make his move yet? Jessie had no idea, and the uncertainty made her want to scream.

"I see you had the same idea we did." Honoria glanced down at their teacups.

Stifling the unworthy impulse to ask her what her first clue was, Jessie pasted an insincere smile on her face and said, "Yes."

Gracefully, Natalie sank down into a sofa across from them and, after a momentary pause, Honoria sat beside her.

"You can have tea, Honoria," Natalie said. "I intend to have a sour-apple martini followed by a second one. I must have walked five miles today. Just look at my poor feet."

Natalie stretched out one long, perfectly formed leg and rotated her foot with its delicate strappy sandals, giving Max ample time to admire her.

"Next time you go for a walk, you ought to try walking shoes," Jessie offered with saccharine sweetness.

Natalie gave an exaggerated shudder. "How unfeminine."

"What? Walking?" Jessie shot back, knowing she should keep quiet but unable to resist the jab.

"I was referring to walking shoes. They are so…so chunky."

Jessie swallowed a nasty crack. Instead she got to her feet. If she stuck around a minute longer she'd undoubtedly say something really bitchy, and that might set Max to wondering why she disliked Natalie so much. And she most emphatically didn't want him to do that.

"Excuse me," Jessie said. "I need to visit the ladies' room. I'll be right back."

"I'll come with you," Honoria said, scotching Jessie's plan to have a few minutes alone.

"I'm sorry we interrupted you," Honoria said as they walked across the lobby, "but once Natalie caught sight of Max there was no stopping her. At least, not by any means that would pass muster in the lobby of a busy hotel. I've known her since preschool, and she isn't as…as bad as she sometimes acts. It's just that her ego took a pretty bad beating when her husband divorced her last winter to marry his pregnant secretary."

"That would tend to deflate one," Jessie said, wishing Honoria would shut up. She didn't want to feel guilty about disliking Natalie. She just wanted her to go away.

"I'll say! Poor Natalie had no idea the jerk was cheating on her. So now she's busy trying to prove that just because her husband preferred a twenty-year-old with a bust size bigger than her IQ doesn't mean that other men don't find her attractive.

"And you must admit that attracting someone of Max

Sheridan's stature would give her a great deal of confidence." Honoria chuckled. "It would also put her ex-husband's nose permanently out of joint."

"Actually, who Max dates is no concern of mine," Jessie said, lying through her teeth. "I really do only have a business relationship with him. Not that he isn't a very nice man," she added on a more cheerful note as she suddenly realized that Honoria wouldn't be so blasé about Natalie's attempt to come on to Max if Honoria were interested in him herself, would she? But if she wasn't interested in Max, then why had she been in his office earlier in the week?

Jessie was mentally running through various ways to ask Honoria about that visit without sounding like either a jealous woman or a busybody when Honoria brought it up herself.

"Max makes even *my* heart beat a little faster," Honoria said. "When I stopped by his office, he made a very generous donation to the animal shelter and never even complained that I was interrupting his work, the way some men would."

"Even yours?" Jessie asked, telling herself that she wasn't indulging her own curiosity. She was doing what Max wanted her to. Finding out what the women he might be interested in thought of him.

"Hmm." Honoria pushed open the door to the ladies' room. "I fell fathoms deep in love years ago. Unfortunately, the man I love married someone else. I keep telling myself that if I can't have the man I want, I should learn to want the man I can have."

"A neat trick if you can do it," Jessie said, wondering if Honoria meant that she was going to try to learn to love Max. But before Jessie could figure out a way to ask, two other women came in and the opportunity for private conversation was lost.

Jessie washed her hands and leaned closer to the mirror, studying her reflection in the plate-glass mirror. She was far too pale and her lipstick had long since disappeared and her eyes…looked haunted. She grimaced. Whoever said love was liberating needed their head examined. She had been much happier before she'd fallen victim to her hopeless passion for Max.

Or had she? Blindly she reached for a hand towel. Had she been happy or had she merely been existing? It was as if she'd spent her entire life listening to a poor-quality recording of her favorite Ninth Symphony by Beethoven and then suddenly found herself plunked down in the middle of the London Philharmonic Orchestra complete with the Mormon Tabernacle Choir. They might be performing the same piece of music as her recording, but now the notes rang pure and clear with a hundred nuances for the listener to enjoy. Her love for Max had done that to her life. He'd brought depth and color and texture to it that hadn't been there before.

And when he left he was going to take it all with him, flinging her back into a cold, gray world. And there was nothing she could do about it. She couldn't make Max fall in love with her, no matter how much she wanted him to. And even if by some miracle he did, then what? She knew it wouldn't last. She didn't have what it took to inspire long-term devotion in anyone. Plus, there was the problem of kids. Did she dare have them and run the risk of them turning out to be alcoholics or junkies like the rest of her relatives? Her ever-present fear surfaced.

Although hers wasn't the only family with a propensity toward addictive personalities. She frowned slightly as she remembered what Max had said about his parents. And Honoria's grandfather had been an alcoholic, and her father had been a compulsive gambler and, if she'd correctly interpreted what had been said at that dinner for the arts, her mother was a shopaholic. And yet Jessie had seen no sign that either Max or Honoria had any intention of allowing their relatives' addictive behavior to shape their own plans for the future. Why not? Because they were braver than she was or more foolhardy?

Automatically dropping a tip on the attendant's plate, Jessie followed Honoria out of the ladies' room.

When she got back to Max, it was to find him smiling faintly at Natalie, who was sipping a drink.

What had happened while she'd been gone? Jessie wondered uneasily. Had Max asked Natalie out? It was certainly what the woman had been angling for. Jessie felt anger spark to life in her chest. She didn't care what kind of emotional havoc Natalie's ex-husband had put her through. Natalie had no business messing with Max's mind. Or any other part of him.

"Ah, there you are." Max got to his feet as they approached. "It's time we were leaving, Jessie. We're meeting Leaverson at the house in fifteen minutes."

Jessie blinked. This was the first she'd heard of the appointment. She stole a quick glance at him, wondering if he'd just made it up to escape Natalie. The possibility raised her spirits.

"I'm ready." Jessie gave him a bright smile.

"Can I beg a ride with you? I'm only going a quarter mile north of there." Natalie smiled hopefully at Max, reminding Jessie of a crocodile trying to look harmless. "And it takes forever to get a cab at this time of day."

"We'd be delighted to drop you off," Max said politely.

"Thank you so much." Natalie hurriedly gulped down the rest of her martini.

"Honoria—" Max turned to her "—may we give you a lift, too?"

"No, thanks," Honoria said. "I've been promising my-self a cream cake all afternoon, but I am glad I ran into you two. I'm hostessing a party for Gerrick Saturday night, and I hope you and Jessie will come."

Don't accept, Jessie willed Max. *Invent some other invi-tation.* Unfortunately, her mental telepathy wasn't working.

"We'll be there, won't we, Jessie?" Max said.

"I look forward to it," Jessie said, trying to infuse some sincerity into her voice.

Jessie nodded a polite goodbye to Honoria and then silently accompanied Max and the chattering Natalie across the crowded lobby toward the hotel's entrance. The doorman ushered them outside and then hurried across the sidewalk to open the Mercedes's door for them.

"Hi, Fred," Jessie said as she scooted across the backseat to the far window.

"Afternoon, Ms. Martinelli," Fred responded absently, his attention focused on Natalie as she gracefully slipped in after Jessie.

"Natalie, this is Fred, my driver. Fred, Natalie."

"Madam," Fred said politely.

Natalie gave him a regal dip of her head and turned to Max. "I do so appreciate you giving me a ride."

Jessie caught Fred's eye and was surprised to see the flash of humor there. Fred had instantly seen through Natalie, so why couldn't Max? Probably because Natalie had dismissed Fred like yesterday's newspaper while she all but drooled on Max.

Jessie huddled against the door as far away from Natalie

and her overwhelming perfume as she could get and prayed that they didn't get caught in a traffic jam. She wanted Natalie out of the car as soon as possible.

"How are your plans for the renovation coming along, Max?" Natalie asked.

"They're coming," Max responded politely.

"I mentioned your brownstone to old Mrs. Adams. You know, the Newport Adamses. And you'll never guess what she told me."

Natalie laid her hand on his thigh and peered up at him through her lashes.

Max felt the pressure of her fingers through the fine wool of his suit pants, and that was all he felt. Other than a feeling of annoyance that she felt free to touch him. Thoughtfully, he studied the classic perfection of Natalie's perfectly made-up face. It left him cold. He wasn't even curious about what it would feel like to kiss her. And yet Jessie...

Max shot a quick glance at Jessie to find her staring out the car window, as if she were mentally distancing herself from him. A gust of anger surged through him. She had no business shutting him out.

"She said she grew up in that house," Natalie said as her hand inched farther up his thigh.

Natalie would definitely benefit from one of Jessie's workshops, Max thought. Somewhere in that impressive list of etiquette rules Jessie was forever quoting at him there had to be an injunction against feeling up one's fellow passengers.

Max grabbed Natalie's hand and dropped it into her lap.

Natalie gave him a conspiratorial smile that exasperated him and said, "You can have Frank drop me off at the next corner."

"*Fred,* would you stop at the next corner?" Max said, carefully keeping his voice neutral.

"With pleasure," Fred said, and Jessie hastily swallowed a grin. That made two of them who couldn't wait to get rid of Natalie.

Once Natalie was gone, Jessie said, "Do you really have an appointment with Leaverson?"

Max gave her a shocked look. "Do you think I'd lie?"

Jessie thought a moment and then said, "Yes."

Max chuckled. "You're right, but in this case I didn't. We really do have an appointment."

"That was kind of interesting," Jessie said slowly.

"What? That I'd lie?"

"No, that old Mrs. Adams grew up in your house. She must be in her nineties, which means that her folks probably lived there early in the last century."

A dreamy expression crossed Jessie's face, and Max had a sudden urge to kiss her. To deepen her expression to ecstasy.

"They would have given balls and fancy dinners. I can just see Mrs. Adams as a debutante sweeping down that gorgeous staircase. There's something so romantic about long dresses and staircases…" Jessie's voice trailed away as she remembered Scarlett O'Hara on the staircase at Tara.

"Not to me. Romantic to me is something a whole lot more physical. Kind of along the lines of…" Max gave in to his almost overpowering urge to touch her. Reaching across the seat, he yanked her toward him with a hunger he made no attempt to hide.

As her soft body landed against him, the floral scent she always wore engulfed him, coloring his thoughts. His heartbeat lurched violently and then began to pound against his rib cage. Suddenly it was a challenge to breathe, but he didn't care. Didn't care about anything but getting as close to Jessie as humanly possible. His arms instinctively tightened as if trying to meld her slender body into his.

His large hand speared through her tumbled curls, holding her head still as he covered her mouth. Excitement exploded in him as he ran the tip of his tongue over her closed lips. He felt her lips part and his tongue plunged inside to explore the tender recesses of her mouth.

The heady taste of her poured through his reeling mind, making him shake. He wanted more. Much more. He wanted to slip his hand beneath her clothes and caress her satiny skin. He wanted…

"Umm." The sound of Fred clearing his throat finally penetrated the hunger raging through Max. Reluctantly he released Jessie, reveling in her flushed, dazed expression. He wasn't sure exactly what she was feeling, but whatever it was, it was pretty powerful. Maybe almost as powerful as what he felt every time he took her in his arms.

"Why did you do that?" Jessie muttered, and then wished she hadn't asked the question. It sounded so incredibly naive. As if a man had to have a reason for kissing a woman.

"Because you are eminently kissable." Max dropped a quick kiss on the end of her nose and then opened the door of the car.

Eminently kissable? Jessie pondered his words as she followed him toward Mr. Leaverson, who was poking at the frames on the basement-level windows with a silver tool of some kind.

Exactly what kind of compliment was that? she wondered. *Sexy* would have been better. *Irresistibly sexy* would have been best. And that kiss he'd just dropped on her nose had been… She tried to analyze it. It had seemed almost tender, but was tender good? She stifled a sigh. She simply didn't know. Max was not an easy man to read.

"Good afternoon." Mr. Leaverson gave them a warm smile. "I have good news for you," he said as Max unlocked the front door.

"I found a craftsman in Florence who will be able to totally restore the central staircase, as well as repair the crown molding in the living room and the bookcases in the library."

"That's great." Jessie made a determined effort to match his enthusiasm. "Anything as gorgeous as that staircase deserves to be whole again."

She paused right inside the door and stared up at it, a faraway look in her eyes.

"What are you seeing?" Max asked. "Old Mrs. Adams sweeping down it in her debutante finery?"

"No," Jessie said slowly. "Your daughter in her wedding finery coming down to meet you on her way to the church." A shiver chased over her skin as she turned to Max, and for one eerie moment she saw him as he'd look thirty years from now. The lines in his lean face were carved a little deeper, there were distinguished wings of gray in his dark hair and his eyes gleamed with love and pride as he looked up the stairs at his daughter.

Max turned and looked up the stairs, and for a split second he caught sight of a slim young woman wearing a cascading white gown. Through the sheer veil he saw a tumble of bright-red curls. The brilliance of her smile as she looked down at him tugged at his heart.

His daughter looked like Jessie, he realized in shock. And she looked like Jessie because he wanted Jessie to be her mother. Because he loved her. The truth broke over him like a tidal wave, threatening to swamp him. He loved Jessie Martinelli.

So now what? he wondered, uncharacteristically rattled by his unexpected insight. Where did he go from here? He didn't know, but he did know that this wasn't the time to worry about it. He turned toward the architect, who was speaking to him, making a desperate effort to concentrate on something other than his shattering discovery.

Later, he promised himself. After he took Jessie home, he'd go back to his office and try to figure out what to do. He'd never had any trouble before coming up with viable plans for unexpected complications. But he had the feeling that falling in love with Jessie was his biggest complication to date.

Chapter Eleven

On Saturday night, Max's impatient gaze swept the crowd of fashionably dressed people in Gerrick's living room, looking for Jessie. Except for the few minutes he'd been able to spend with Jessie before he'd been cornered by some idiot who'd wanted him to finance a steam engine for cars, the evening had been a total waste of time. Time he could have better spent figuring out what to do about his love for Jessie.

He knew what he wanted to do. He'd figured that out around three o'clock last night. He wanted to marry Jessie and live happily ever after. What he hadn't been able to figure out was how to present the idea to her so that she'd buy into it.

For the first time in his life, he couldn't come up with a plan to accomplish his goals. Hell, he hadn't even been able to come up with a glimmer of an idea, never mind a full-blown plan. The fear of her saying no had shut down his normal creative processes. All he could think about was that if he didn't ask Jessie, she couldn't say no, and if she didn't say no, they could at least continue as they were. He could see her almost daily and occasionally kiss her. But he could only do that if he pretended to still be looking for a wife. The thought grated. He didn't want his relationship with Jessie to be based on a lie.

Maybe he could… A man moved, and he caught sight of Jessie's bright-red hair. He headed straight for her.

"How much longer do we have to stay?" he whispered in a low aside.

Jessie shot a quick glance around, hoping that no one had overheard him. "Another half hour should do it."

"That's an eternity. Why don't we just sneak out the back way and go to my place," he said. If he could just get her alone, maybe the right words to tell her how he felt would come. At the very least, he could kiss her. That wouldn't solve anything, but it would sure make him feel better.

"Jessie." Gerrick hurried up to them. "Siefert from the big mutual fund would like to meet you."

Jessie blinked in confusion. "Me? Why?"

Gerrick grinned at her. "He wants to pump you about Saudi business manners and, if I know Tom, he'll try to get the information without paying for it. Don't let him."

Jessie smiled back. "Don't worry. I've had lots of experience with his type."

"Come on. I'll introduce you," Gerrick said.

"Good luck," Max told her when she turned to him to make sure he didn't mind her doing business on his time.

Thirty minutes later, Jessie left Siefert with the promise to call his office and set up an appointment to give his top executives a workshop on Middle Eastern manners. Elated about the unexpected bit of business, she glanced around, looking for Max.

She couldn't find him in the living room, the family room or the library, so she headed toward the kitchen, where earlier some of the men had been huddled around the wine cooler discussing the Yankees.

Halfway down the hallway, Jessie heard the deep rumble of Max's voice coming from behind a partially open door to her right.

"...I'd need to see the specs before I could even say whether I would be interested in seeing more," Jessie heard Max say.

It sounded like a business discussion, Jessie decided, and it couldn't be more private. Max had been very specific about the fact that he never discussed confidential business matters at parties.

She reached out to push open the door and then froze when she heard Honoria's voice say, "Fair enough. There's a second thing I want to talk to you about.

"I've thought and thought about how to put this, and finally decided that the best way would be to simply come right out with it. I hope that you'll be as straightforward with your answer."

Jessie stood as if welded to the spot behind the door, knowing she should leave but unable to move. Fear of what Honoria might say held her pinned in place.

"I may be reading the signs wrong, Max," Honoria said, "but I think you've reached a point in your life when you're actively looking for a wife. If that's so, I'd like to apply for the role. I'm thirty years old, and I've long since given up expecting to fall madly in love. What did they used to call them? Marriages of convenience? I really think you and I could make a success of one."

"Honoria," Max said, and Jessie shivered at the tender note she could hear in his voice. Pain lanced through her, ripping her loose from the strange inertia that had gripped her. She shouldn't be standing here eavesdropping on their private conversation. The though surfaced through the maelstrom of emotion tearing through her. She might love Max, but that didn't give her the right to violate his privacy. With an almost physical act of will, Jessie forced herself to move away. Thankfully, the restroom was free and she was able to lock herself in while she struggled to regain control of her shredded emotions.

She'd known from the very beginning that this would happen eventually, she reminded herself. The whole purpose behind her being with Max was to help him find a wife. And she wasn't going to cry because he had, she ordered herself as she saw a tear tracking down her face. She had no right to cry. She hadn't lost Max, because Max had never been hers in the first place. Not in any meaningful sense of the word.

Jessie jerked the cold-water faucet on and stuck her hands under the chilly flow. The cold water helped her to regain her composure. She could get through this, she told herself. She was strong. Life had made her that way. She'd go back into that party and act for all she was worth. No one, least of all Max, would ever know how much she was hurting.

Ten minutes later she emerged from the bathroom and went into the living room.

To her surprise Max and Honoria were both there, and they weren't together. Max was standing by the bar, listening to a thin man who was earnestly expounding on something or other, while Honoria was talking to the caterer.

Why weren't they celebrating their decision to marry? Probably because Honoria's duties as hostess interfered,

Jessie figured. After all, they'd have the rest of their lives to spend together. The thought made her want to start crying, and she clenched her teeth together and stared fixedly at a modern painting on the wall while she struggled for control. Its jagged lines of red, crimson and hot pink fit her mood of faint desperation exactly.

"There you are." Max's deep voice made her jump. "I looked for you and couldn't find you."

"I was in the bathroom," Jessie said. Despite her efforts to sound normal, her voice came out thin and tense.

Max frowned slightly as he studied her pale features. "Are you okay?"

"Yes. Who was the man you were talking to?" Jessie grabbed the first topic she could think of to change the subject.

"Jim Franchetti. He had some interesting insights on the European Union. How about if we leave now?"

"Leave?" Jessie repeated blankly, looking around for Honoria. She was still deep in discussion with the caterer. Max had been discussing marriage with Honoria ten minutes before, and now he wanted to go? Was that how businesslike marriages were handled? Jessie shivered. If she were lucky enough to be engaged to Max, she'd stick to him like glue.

"As in 'exit the premises,'" Max said. "Are you sure you're okay? You sound disoriented, and you're really pale."

"I have a headache," Jessie said. Under normal circumstances she would never lie to get out of her social obligations, but these were hardly normal circumstances. She had to escape before she broke down.

"Come on." Max put a protective arm around her shoulders and steered her toward the door.

"We have to say goodbye to our hosts and thank them for the evening," Jessie said, when what she really wanted to do was consign both Farringtons to outer Mongolia.

"To hell with…" Max broke off as Gerrick noticed them moving toward the door and hurried to them.

"You aren't leaving already, are you?" Gerrick asked.

"Yes." Max's curt voice made it clear the subject was not open for discussion. "Give me a call, and we'll set up an appointment to talk."

Jessie felt a sharp stab of pain at Max's words. He must want to talk to Gerrick about marrying his sister. Unless possibly it was about Gerrick's biotech start-up?

"I'll do that," Gerrick assured him as he opened the front door for them. "Take care," he called as they left.

Jessie stumbled slightly as they stepped into the elevator, and Max instinctively steadied her against his body. Even though she knew it was a bad idea, she couldn't resist the temptation to relax into him. She would probably never get the chance to touch him again. Max was not the kind of man to cheat on a woman, and now that he was engaged to Honoria…

The thought of his engagement sent a wave of pain crashing through her. She made a valiant effort to shut it out and concentrate on getting home without letting him see just how upset she was.

Fred was double-parked at the curb, and Jessie climbed into the car, her movements stiff with the effort of holding in all her churning emotions.

"My apartment isn't far from here," Max said. "Why don't we stop there and get you something for your headache? We can have a cup of coffee and talk."

Jessie hastily gulped back her horrified refusal. She absolutely couldn't face Max telling her about his plans now. She needed some time to erect her defenses so she could take his dismissal with a calm detachment that wouldn't betray how the knowledge was tearing her apart. It shouldn't take her more than ten or twenty years, she thought with grim humor.

"Thanks, but I'd rather go home. All I need is a good night's sleep. I'll be fine in the morning."

"Okay." To her relief, he didn't argue.

Jessie leaned back in the seat and closed her eyes, resisting the impulse to steal peeks at Max. To hoard images of his dear face against a bleak future that didn't include him.

"Here we are," Max said as Fred pulled up in front of Jessie's apartment house. "Are you sure you don't want me to come up with you?"

"I'll be fine." Jessie repeated the words like a mantra.

"Good night, Fred. Thanks for the evening, Max," she said as she climbed out of the car with more haste than finesse.

"If you need anything, call me. I'll be home tonight and in the office most of the day tomorrow, working with Pearsall. I'll see you in my office at ten Monday morning."

"Ten o'clock Monday morning," Jessie repeated, wishing there was some way to handle her dismissal over the phone. Or, better yet, by mail. But if she refused to meet him, he'd realize that she was emotionally involved, and her pride wouldn't allow that. Her pride was all she had left. She was determined to leave him with an intact image of her as a competent professional.

"Good night, Max." With a fleeting smile that she was hard-pressed to hang on to, she hurried into her apartment building. Maybe she'd get lucky and the world would end before Monday and solve all her problems.

Sunday morning dawned bright and clear in direct opposition to the bleak feelings of desolation that filled her. Jessie had repeated every single positive affirmation that she had taped on the refrigerator and not one of them had made her feel any better. Probably because she knew that everything wasn't going to be all right.

Jessie was working on her second cup of coffee and staring blankly at the Sunday comics when the phone rang. She glanced at the caller ID. It appeared to be a residential phone out on the Island, but she didn't recognize it. Was it one of the people she'd met last night at Gerrick's party? Someone who wanted to ask her about workshops?

Jessie picked up the phone and then wished she hadn't when she heard her mother's voice.

"Jessie, please don't hang up. I need to talk to you."

The faintly desperate voice resonated through Jessie. Her mother sounded the way she felt. As if she knew that she didn't have a hope in hell of winning but was determined to see it through to the bitter end. Could talking to her really mean that much to her mother? Jessie wondered dubiously.

It had been what…? Almost two weeks since she'd first written. Two weeks of staying on target had to be some kind of record for her mother.

"Jessie, I've changed." Her mother rushed into speech. "I'm clean. I made myself wait a year after I got out of jail before I contacted you to prove that I could live on the outside without junk. I've got a good job. I'm the housekeeper for a couple of parish priests out on the Island. I have a nice little apartment above the garage and a savings account and everything. Everything but my daughter. Please give me another chance."

Jessie rubbed her forehead, which ached from her sleepless night. Bitter experience with her mother was urging her to refuse to have anything to do with her, but she simply couldn't bring herself to inflict any more pain, even in self-defense.

"All right, I'll meet you, and we can talk. But that's all I'm promising," she added as her mother started to thank her. "When are you free?"

"I'm off on Tuesday and Wednesday. Things are pretty busy around here on the weekends."

Not Tuesday, Jessie thought. After Max told her about his upcoming marriage on Monday, she would be in no shape to do anything on Tuesday. "Wednesday works for me," Jessie finally said. "How about meeting on the steps of the Met about one. We can find a bench in there and talk."

"Wednesday at one," her mother repeated. "And thank you, Jessie."

"We'll see. Bye." Jessie hung up and sagged back into her chair, wondering if she had lost her mind. She knew she shouldn't have anything to do with her mother, but somehow she'd sounded so miserable and…and it didn't seem to matter now that Max was about to go out of her life. Nothing mattered. Jessie sniffed back tears, refusing to cry. Modern women didn't cry over men.

Besides, she thought glumly, there was still the world-might-end option. She had one more night to hope.

Not surprisingly, Monday was another obscenely bright day, which almost seemed to mock her feelings of impending disaster.

Nine-fifty found Jessie in the lobby of Max's office building, mentally trying to psych herself up to face him. She could do it, she assured herself. All she had to do was hang on to her professional front like grim death while she listened to him tell her about how he was going to marry Honoria. Then she would offer him a quick congratulations, plead another appointment and beat a fast retreat.

Determinedly Jessie entered the empty elevator and forced herself to punch the button for the fifty-second floor. She could do this. She…

Suppose Honoria was there with Max! The truly appalling possibility occurred to her. How could she smile and say the right things if she had to watch the two of them together?

She would worry about that if and when it happened, she decided. There was no sense borrowing trouble. She had enough as it was.

The elevator doors opened on the fifty-second floor, and Jessie forced her trembling legs to carry her across the thick carpeting to the receptionist, who was on the phone. The woman gave her a warm smile and silently mouthed, *He's expecting you.*

Taking a deep breath, Jessie headed for Max's office.

His door was open, and she paused in the hallway, allowing herself the luxury of simply looking at his beloved features for a moment. He was seated at his desk, talking on the phone. Catching sight of her, he pointed at the chair in front of his desk.

Jessie surreptitiously glanced around the spacious office as she entered. To her relief, Honoria was nowhere to be seen. At least that was one complication she wouldn't have to deal with.

Jessie gingerly perched on the chair and resumed her deep breathing.

"You still look pale." Max's words came out almost like an accusation.

"It's hot outside, and I was hurrying so as not to be late."

"Not necessary. I'd have waited."

"Oh," Jessie mumbled, wondering how to get him to the reason he'd asked her to come. She couldn't come right out and admit she knew about him and Honoria, because then she'd have to admit she'd been eavesdropping on their private conversation. And while he had told her to eavesdrop, she knew full well he hadn't meant on him.

* * *

Max resisted the powerful urge to snatch her up in his arms and try to erase the bleakness in her eyes. But before he could do that, he needed to talk to her. To tell her how much he loved her. To convince her to let him teach her to love him. Then, if she agreed, he could take her back to his apartment. If she didn't… A momentary doubt shook him, but he refused to allow it to grow. Jessie liked him. They had fun together, and she certainly responded to his kisses. There was a very powerful chemistry between them. He could build on that.

Nervously Jessie watched as Max stood up and walked around his desk, stopping inches from her. She didn't want him close to her. When he was close to her, she forgot everything but how much she loved him.

"Jessie," Max said. "I want… That is, you've come to mean… Oh, to hell with it. Will you marry me?" he blurted out.

"What!" Jessie stared at him, not sure she'd really heard that or if her wishful thinking had somehow conjured the words out of her imagination.

"I want to marry you," he repeated.

"But…why?" she finally got out.

"Because you're everything any sane man could want in a woman. You're kind and sexy and intelligent and compassionate. I admire how hard you've worked to carve out a business niche that's uniquely yours. I'm proud of what you've done professionally, and I'd never ask you to give it up. I figure if we both cut back on work a little, we could easily manage two or three kids. Both of us are very good at organization."

* * *

Max paused when he realized he was not getting a response from her. He'd never proposed to a woman before, but it seemed to him that a woman should be showing a little enthusiasm at this point.

His stomach lurched as fear chilled his skin. She was going to turn him down.

Jessie stared down at her clasped hands and tried to reconcile his proposal with the conversation she'd overheard last night. She couldn't. He couldn't be asking her on the rebound, because Honoria had been the one to propose to him. But if he were asking her to marry him, that meant he had turned Honoria down. But why? Honoria was exactly what he'd said he wanted in a wife. Right down to the blond hair. What had happened to change his mind about the type of woman he wanted to marry?

She hadn't realized she said the words aloud until Max responded.

"I grew up," he said. "When I came up with the idea of the perfect wife and mother, I was just a teenager. My ideal was a combination of information gleaned from television, the movies, my friends' mothers and bits I'd read in the society pages. I wanted a wife who would show them all that I was the best. Kind of the ultimate trophy that I could wave at everyone and say, 'Hey, look at me. I've arrived.'

"When I decided it was time to marry, I automatically slipped my old ideas into the slot called 'Wife.' It really didn't take me long to realize that I didn't want to marry some abstract quality, I wanted to marry you.

"Say something," he ordered when she sat hunched in her chair.

"You can't marry me." She forced the words out, trying not to let him see how much they hurt her. "You want kids, and I can't have them."

"I want kids in part because they'd be yours," Max said. "But I want you first and last. If you can't have kids, then we'll adopt a few. There are plenty in the world who could use a good home."

"It's not that." Jessie stared down at her hands, rather surprised to find that they were tightly clenched.

"Then what is it? There's nothing you could have ever done that would change how I feel about you."

A bitter laugh escaped Jessie. "I'll have to introduce you to my mother sometime."

"What are you talking about? Your mother must be rather special if she raised you."

"My mother didn't raise me. I doubt she gave me a thought from one month to the next. My mother was an alcoholic and a drug addict. Normally she supported her habits with prostitution, but when I was fourteen she took up selling crack." Jessie forced herself to tell him the bitter truth about her background. "One of her first sales was to an undercover agent. She went to jail, and I was put in foster care. I hadn't heard a word from her until the first day I met with you. She wrote and said she wanted to establish a relationship with me, and I told her to go away and leave me alone, but she wouldn't," Jessie said. "She kept reappearing and saying she'd changed."

Max grimaced. "My mother used that line every time she wanted me to do something. She invariably got drunk and forgot about it."

"Yeah. I know how that one goes. But despite all that, I've agreed to meet with her Wednesday afternoon."

"I can come with you. Sometimes a third party can keep everything from getting too intense. All I have scheduled that day is a morning appointment with Gerrick to talk about my investing in his start-up."

Jessie felt something inside her warm at his offer. "Thanks, anyway, but I think this is something I have to face myself."

Max scooped her out of the chair and then sat back down with her in his lap. His arms tightened around her, and he tucked her head beneath his chin.

Jessie could hear the steady beat of his heart in her ear, and she found the sound infinitely comforting.

"You don't ever have to face anything alone again unless you choose to," Max said flatly. "I love you, and I want to marry you. Everything else is just a side issue. An unimportant side issue."

Jessie tensed as his totally unexpected words poured over her, stealing her breath and making her skin tingle.

"You love me?" she blurted out.

"I think I fell in love with you the minute I set eyes on you. I took one look at you and wanted to leap over my desk and grab you and never let go. You turned me on so hard and so fast I had trouble remembering why you were even there.

"I told myself it was just lust, and it would fade. But it wasn't, and it didn't. The more I got to know you, the deeper in love I fell."

"You really love me?" Jessie whispered.

"I really love you." Max repeated the words like a vow. "I want to marry you and spend the rest of my life making you happy."

"But my background…"

"I wouldn't change a single thing about your past, because it's made you what you are. And I don't give a damn what anybody but you thinks. All I want is that you let me teach you how to love me."

Jessie stared into his tense features and blurted out, "You don't have to teach me anything. I already love you. I've loved you for ages. Oh, Max, I've been so unhappy thinking you were going to marry someone else and I'd never see you again. When you bought that necklace, I thought you'd decided on Honoria."

"I bought that necklace because the stones reminded me of your eyes. I had some vague idea of giving it to you along with your bonus."

Jessie threw her arms around his neck, reveling in the freedom to touch him. "I don't want anything but you. You're absolutely perfect."

Max chuckled, and the happy sound reverberated through her. "Hardly, but I'm willing to work at it."

Jessie snuggled deeper into his embrace. "About kids, Max. It isn't that I don't want any. It's that I'm afraid to have them. My family is so deep in addictive tendencies… What if I pass them on to my kids?"

"We got our genes from our massively dysfunctional parents, and we turned out okay. Our kids are going to be even less at risk 'cause they'll have us to look out for them and teach them how to handle stress."

"But that's part of the problem. I haven't a clue about how to raise a kid. I have no personal experience to draw on."

"Sure, you do. Think of what you do at the center. Think of Luis and how well you did in mentoring him."

"I guess. But suppose I make mistakes?"

"I will admit, that scenario had me pretty worried at first, but the more I thought about it, the more I realized that every new parent is going to make mistakes. It goes with the territory. The important thing is that we'll love them. Besides, I didn't know anything about business when I started out, and look where I wound up."

Jessie glanced around the spacious office with its priceless antiques.

"I will admit that's a pretty convincing argument," she conceded. "And we can always buy a book on parenting."

"I'll buy you a whole damn bookstore if you want. But the best thing we have going for us as parents is that the kid won't have anything to compare us with. And by the time he's old enough to notice, we'll be old hands at it."

"You make it all sound so easy," Jessie said wistfully.

"It is easy," Max said as he pulled her closer. "I love you, and you love me. In the final analysis, that's all that matters."

Jessie smiled blindingly at him.

* * * * *

SILHOUETTE Romance®

COMING NEXT MONTH

#1818 CHASING DREAMS—Cara Colter
Book-smart and reserved, Jessica King instinctively knows she
needs someone to bring her inner wild child out. And though she's
engaged to a somewhat stuffy academic, something tells her that
earthy mechanic Garner Blake, whom she has just met, may be
more the man of her dreams…. But can she find the courage now to
listen to her heart and not her head?

#1819 WISHING AND HOPING—Susan Meier
Word on the street is that Tia Capriotti is suddenly marrying
Drew Wallace, a longtime neighbor *and* her father's best friend. But
inquiring minds want to know—is there something political afoot in
their courtship? And what is that subtle bulge at her belly?

#1820 IF THE SLIPPER FITS—Elizabeth Harbison
Concierge; browbeaten orphan—they might be one and the same,
with the way Prince Conrad's stepmother treats hostess Lily Tilden
in her own boutique hotel. To uncover the jewel that is hers and
Conrad's love, Lily must first overcome the royal tricks of this
woman, who seems to have studied carefully the wicked women
of yore!

#1821 THE PARENT TRAP—Lissa Manley
Divorcée Jill Lindstrom and widower Brandon Clark each just
wanted to leave hectic lives and open landmark restaurants in the
small Oregon town. But their cooking mixtures seem bland when
compared to the elaborate schemes their daughters concoct to give
the pair a taste of how delicious their lives could be together….

SRCNM0506